The Riddle in the Rare Book

Nancy turned on the radio to keep herself company as she started down the old river road. She was feeling tired, so she turned the radio up louder.

I wish I'd gotten a cup of coffee, she thought drowsily. It wasn't very late, but she was having a hard time keeping her eyes open. She felt a little strange.

Then, as Nancy took a curve on the rain-slick road, she felt herself go into a skid. Steer into it, she told herself, but she couldn't seem to react quickly enough. Everything had slowed down as though it were some awful dream.

She could feel the car sliding sideways, but she felt powerless, unable to stop it. Next she heard a massive crashing sound. The car bounced hard and rolled onto its side.

Then everything went black.

Nancy Drew
Mystery Stories

Available from MINSTREL Books

NANCY DREW MYSTERY STORIES®

126

NANCY DREW®

THE RIDDLE IN THE RARE BOOK

CAROLYN KEENE

A MINSTREL® BOOK

Published by POCKET BOOKS
New York   London   Toronto   Sydney   Singapore

A MINSTREL PAPERBACK *Original*

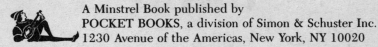

A Minstrel Book published by
POCKET BOOKS, a division of Simon & Schuster Inc.
1230 Avenue of the Americas, New York, NY 10020

Copyright © 1995 by Simon & Schuster Inc.
Produced by Mega-Books, Inc.

ISBN: 0-671-87209-5

First Minstrel Books printing August 1995

10   9   8   7   6

NANCY DREW, NANCY DREW MYSTERY STORIES, A MINSTREL BOOK and colophon are registered trademarks of Simon & Schuster Inc.

Cover art by Aleta Jenks

Printed in the U.S.A.

Contents

1

Stolen!

"I don't believe it!" Nancy Drew said, stopping in surprise in the middle of the sidewalk.

Before her, dozens of people swarmed around the steps of the old First River Heights Bank, which had recently been converted into Bloom's Bookstore & Coffeehouse. "Are all those people really waiting for a poetry reading?" Nancy asked her friend Bess Marvin.

"Of course," Bess said. "This is going to be a fantastically exciting evening!"

"How can a poetry reading be fantastically exciting?" George Fayne asked skeptically.

"These new coffeehouses are supposed to be *the* place to meet cute guys," Bess explained. "And remember, I haven't had a date in two whole weeks."

George laughed and said, "I should have known it was something like that."

Tall and slender, with reddish-blond hair,

Nancy had been best friends for years with Bess and George. Though they looked nothing alike, Bess and George were first cousins. George was slim and athletic with short brown hair and dark eyes. Bess had straight blond hair and blue eyes and was far more interested in clothes and guys than her cousin was.

Bess waved a glossy flyer at them. "We're so lucky Richard Munro is reading tonight."

"Who is Richard Munro?" Nancy asked.

"Only the most devastatingly handsome poet on earth," Bess replied. "Black hair, green eyes, cheekbones to die for—"

"Sounds like he meets all the requirements for a great poet," George said dryly. "Can he write?"

"Of course he can," Bess said indignantly.

"Come on, you two," Nancy said, laughing. "Let's go inside and see for ourselves."

Nancy liked Bloom's the moment she walked in the door. With its marble floors, wood-paneled walls, and carved stone columns, the old bank building had once been imposing. But the new owners had totally transformed it, adding a cheerful clutter of books and antique furniture. Bookcases divided the space into cozy little corners, with tables and a mismatched assortment of loveseats and old velvet armchairs. Oriental rugs were scattered on the marble floor, which not only made the room quieter, but also gave it a warmer atmosphere.

Nancy saw that Bess was right: Bloom's *was* the new hot place in River Heights. The coffeehouse was crowded with young people, all browsing the bookshelves or talking and laughing at the tables.

Bess led the way to the coffee bar, where she eyed the tempting pastries.

"What about your diet?" Nancy teased her.

"I'm starting tomorrow," Bess said firmly.

George rolled her eyes at Nancy. Bess was always starting "tomorrow."

"Look! Over there!" Bess said in a dramatic whisper. When Nancy and George glanced to their right, where Bess was pointing, she said urgently, "No, don't turn around! Don't be obvious. It's him."

"Him who?" George asked, still searching the room.

"Richard Munro, the poet," Bess said with a sigh. "Isn't he gorgeous? Let's get some coffee and go sit near him."

George groaned, but there was no arguing with Bess. The three girls filled a tray with coffee and cakes and took it over to the corner of the room, where a small raised platform had been set up for readings. Bess smiled brightly at the handsome young poet as she sat down on the chair closest to him, but he was about six feet away and didn't look up from the book he was poring over.

Just then a tall woman in her late teens approached the girls' table. She had long black hair, almond eyes, and a sprinkling of freckles across her nose. "George, is that you?" she asked.

George looked up and smiled. "Lori Chang! I haven't seen you in ages. Why don't you join us?"

"I'd love to," Lori said.

George introduced Lori to Nancy and Bess. "Her mother plays tennis with my mom," George explained.

"Hi, Nancy, Bess," Lori said.

With difficulty, Bess pulled her gaze away from Richard Munro. Lori noticed this and laughed. "Oh, you've fallen under the Munro spell, have you?" she said in a low voice to Bess. "Well, look out. He's trouble."

"What kind of trouble?" Nancy asked.

"He's got a 'rep,' if you know what I mean," Lori said.

"What kind of reputation?" Bess asked, wide-eyed.

"Oh, you know. Expensive tastes, expensive girlfriends. And a trail of broken hearts wherever he goes," Lori said.

"Better be careful, Bess, or you might be Richard Munro's next victim," George joked.

"Well, maybe he just hasn't found the right girlfriend yet," Bess said.

"He's Cyril Bloom's assistant," Lori explained. "Cyril's the guy who owns the place. He's a real sweetie. There he is, in the corner, with the silver hair and tweed jacket and turtleneck."

"The one with the pipe? Is he a poet, too? He looks just like a poet should look," Bess said.

"Oh yes," Lori said. "He doesn't write anymore, but he was fairly well known about twenty years ago, when his first book of poems was

4

published. Haven't you heard of Cyril Bloom? His book was called *Dark Lady*. He's written several others since then."

Bess shook her head. "I've only just begun to appreciate poetry," she admitted.

"I love poetry," Lori said. "And fiction, history, biographies . . . I'm crazy about books. That's why I work with them now."

"Do you work here at Bloom's, too?" Nancy asked.

Lori shook her head. "No, I'm apprenticed to a master bookbinder," she said. "I'm learning how to bind books and restore old bindings. We do a lot of work for Cyril, repairing rare old editions when they're damaged."

"Old editions?" Nancy asked. "I didn't know Bloom's sold old books. I see only new books here."

Lori pointed to the balcony that ran around the room above their heads. On the balcony were even more bookcases. Nancy could see that the books on the shelves were mostly leather and cloth bound. "That's where the old books are shelved," Lori said. Then she pointed to a wall on the first floor. "And see that counter over there, where the bank tellers used to stand? The really valuable editions are kept in the rare book room behind the old tellers' windows."

"Shhh, you two," Bess said. "I think the reading is starting."

Cyril Bloom stepped up to the microphone on

the platform. After welcoming the crowd, he introduced the three poets who would be reading. All three were lively performers as well as good writers, and Nancy found that the time passed quickly.

Bess, however, fidgeted during the first two readings, then leaned forward in rapt fascination for Richard Munro's. The minute he finished, Bess jumped up, saying, "I've got to tell Richard that I just love his poems."

"And his green eyes and his broad shoulders," George teased her. Bess tossed her head and slipped away.

"I have to be going, George," Lori said. "But it was great seeing you. Here's my number at the bookbinding workshop—let's keep in touch." She handed George a scrap of paper and waved good-bye.

As Lori walked away, George asked Nancy, "Are you in any hurry to leave? I'd like to check out the sports books."

"Go ahead," Nancy said. "I want to look around, too. And it's obvious Bess doesn't want to leave just yet." They had both noticed that Bess had found a seat right beside Richard. She was smiling happily as he entertained a circle of young women.

Nancy wandered over to one of the bank counter windows, where she saw Cyril Bloom standing behind a cash register. "May I see the rare book room, please?" she asked.

"Of course," Cyril said. "I'll unlock the door." As he gave her a charming smile, Nancy thought to herself that he'd probably once broken as many hearts as Richard Munro.

Cyril led Nancy behind the old counter and unlocked the door with a brass key. Nancy was intrigued—discovering what was behind locked doors always appealed to her sense of adventure. They stepped into a little room lined with antique glass-fronted bookcases. The room held the wonderful musty scent of old leather. Many of the books inside had beautiful designs stamped in gold on their spines. Nancy wondered if some of these were books Lori Chang had repaired at the bookbindery.

She circled the room, reading the titles of books of all sizes. Some titles were familiar; some she'd never heard before. Then, in one of the cases, she saw a book she recognized—Arthur Conan Doyle's classic Sherlock Holmes mystery *The Hound of the Baskervilles*. "May I see that?" she asked, pointing to the book.

Cyril took the book out of the case and handed it carefully to Nancy. She looked over the familiar gray dust jacket with the scarlet type, then lifted the jacket to examine the leather cover's embossed design: a hound silhouetted against the moon. It was just like a copy she had at home. A skilled detective, Nancy had been given the book by someone for whom she had solved a case.

Opening the cover, she looked at the price

written on the first page—and almost dropped the book in shock. Two thousand dollars! She had no idea that the book was worth so much.

Thanking Cyril, Nancy handed the book back to him and left the rare book room. She paused on the other side of the counter to look at some paintings by a local artist.

Just then a small, plump middle-aged woman in a garish red-and-purple print dress strode up to the counter. Her heels clicked loudly on the marble floor, and her face was shadowed by her hat's enormous brim. Cyril, who had returned to the cash register behind the counter, looked up in surprise.

The woman in the hat brought her fist down on the counter and announced in a booming voice, "Cyril, I've come for the book you said you were holding for me—the British edition of *Peter Pan in Kensington Gardens*. And mark my words—I'm not paying four hundred for it. Truepenny Books had it listed for two seventy-five in its catalog. Don't think you can pull one over on me after all these years!"

"But, Risa," Cyril said uneasily, "I—I can't sell it to you at all. I'm afraid it's gone."

"What!" the little woman bellowed. "You double-crossing toad! I told you I wanted that copy, and you sold it out from under—"

"I didn't sell it, Risa," Cyril interrupted. "Now, calm down. You see"—he looked around and dropped his voice, but Nancy still heard him say quietly—"it was stolen."

"Stolen?" Risa said loudly.

Cyril winced and said, "Shhh. I don't want this getting around. I don't want people getting the idea that my store's security is lax."

Risa's strident voice softened with sympathy. "Oh, dear. I know just how you feel, Cyril," she said. "Why, I've had two books stolen recently myself. And Gerard lost that rare edition of *Huckleberry Finn* just last week."

Nancy moved a little closer, her heart beating faster. Maybe, she thought excitedly, this was the start of a new mystery for her to solve.

"I don't understand," Risa said. "How could anyone get into that fancy vault of yours?"

"The book wasn't in the vault when it disappeared," Cyril explained. "It had just come back from the bookbinder and—"

The two moved away, and Nancy couldn't hear the rest of their discussion. Should she admit she'd been eavesdropping and break into their private conversation? she wondered, itching with curiosity. But just then she felt a hand on her arm.

"I think we'd better go rescue Bess," George said, "before she does something really dumb."

"Richard Munro?" Nancy guessed.

George nodded. "She's already given him her phone number. I think she's about to ask him to marry her or something."

Nancy and George found Bess sitting on a loveseat next to Richard Munro, balancing a mug of coffee on her knee and gazing at him with starstruck eyes. Nancy had to admit that Richard

9

Munro was handsome, with his high cheekbones and wavy black hair.

"I just adore poetry," Bess was saying. "Especially love poems."

"Hmmm," Richard Munro said.

"Sonnets are my all-time favorites," Bess went on. "They're just so . . . poetic."

Richard gave her a blank stare. George jabbed Nancy with her elbow.

"Bess," Nancy cut in hastily, "I'm sorry to interrupt, but I really have to get home."

Bess turned toward Nancy. "Oh," she murmured, her face crumpling in disappointment.

Richard stood up quickly. "Catch you later," he said, and headed for the coffee bar.

"Did you hear that?" Bess asked dreamily as she rose to her feet. "He wants to see me again."

"Uh, Bess, he didn't exactly say that," Nancy pointed out. She knew that Bess fell in love easily, and she didn't want to see her friend hurt.

"But he does," Bess insisted as the three friends walked to the door. "Don't you remember when Richard read that line about eternal love? He was looking straight at *me* when he read it. There was definitely some serious eye contact happening back there."

"That doesn't prove anything," George said.

Bess looked offended. "You're always so negative, George," she complained. "Your problem is, you're not a romantic. If you had the soul of a poet, like I do, you'd understand."

After leaving Bloom's, Bess strode down Main

Street in a huff. Nancy and George caught up to her next to Nancy's blue Mustang. As Nancy unlocked the car doors, she said to Bess, "The soul of a poet? Is poetry your new passion—I mean, after chocolate, of course." Nancy added the last comment with a laugh.

"Well, chocolate still comes first, I confess," Bess said. "But I've been reading up on poetry ever since I saw the flyer with Richard's picture on it last week."

As it turned out, Bess actually had been reading a lot of poetry. In fact, she talked about poetry nonstop until Nancy dropped her and George off at the Faynes' house.

When Nancy got home, she found her father and Hannah Gruen in the living room, watching the TV news. Hannah, a middle-aged woman with silver gray hair, was the Drews' housekeeper. She'd lived with Nancy and her father ever since Mrs. Drew had died, when Nancy was very young.

"How was Bloom's?" Carson Drew asked.

"Interesting," Nancy answered. "Remember that old *Hound of the Baskervilles* that Branwyn Froud gave me when I found her mother's necklace? I saw one like it in Bloom's that's selling for two thousand dollars."

Hannah's jaw dropped. "Who on earth would pay that much money for a book?" she asked, amazed.

"Book collectors," Carson Drew answered.

"Exactly," Nancy said. Stepping over to the living room shelves, she began to look for her copy

11

of the Sherlock Holmes book. She checked the bookcase behind the wing chair and then the shelves that faced the sofa, with no luck. "I don't see it anywhere," she said.

Mr. Drew stood up and stretched. "Maybe it wound up in my study by mistake," he said. "I'll check there."

"I might as well look, too," Hannah said, switching off the TV. She started to hunt through the bookcase in the hallway while Nancy continued to search the living room.

Twenty minutes later, Nancy, Carson, and Hannah stood puzzled in the front hall. "It's just not here," Hannah said. "We've searched everywhere."

"That's what I was afraid of," Nancy said with a sinking feeling.

"What do you mean?" her father asked.

"There was one other thing I learned at Bloom's tonight," Nancy explained. "It seems that someone in this area is stealing rare books. I'm afraid that my *Hound of the Baskervilles* may be gone for good!"

2

Caught in the Act

Nancy explained to her father and Hannah how Cyril Bloom and Risa had both had rare books stolen recently. "I don't know, Nan," Mr. Drew said doubtfully. "Do you really think someone would break into this house to take one book and nothing else?"

"But it's a two-thousand-dollar book, Dad! And what if the thief specializes in selling to book collectors?" Nancy suggested. "Or maybe the thief *is* a collector looking for certain titles for his own collection."

Hannah sat down heavily on a chair. "And I've always felt so safe in this house," she said, worried.

"You still are," Mr. Drew assured her. "Let's not panic. We don't even know for certain that the book was stolen."

But Nancy's instinct told her that there was a mystery here. "I'm going to call the police and

13

report this," she said. "Maybe they can tell me something about the other book thefts. Maybe there's a link."

Stepping to the phone, Nancy punched in the phone number for the police station. An Officer Nomura answered the phone. Nancy, who knew Nomura from a previous case, explained the case to her.

Officer Nomura listened intently. "Any signs of a break-in at your house?" she finally asked.

"None," Nancy said. "But I'm not sure when the book was stolen. We just discovered that it was missing tonight."

"You're sure you didn't just misplace it?" the officer asked.

"Positive," Nancy said.

"There's not a lot I can do right now besides file this report," Officer Nomura admitted. "I mean, one missing book isn't exactly a big priority. We have much more serious crimes to deal with."

"But it's not just one book," Nancy said. "At Bloom's Bookstore tonight, I heard Cyril Bloom talking about other rare books that have been stolen lately. Do you know anything about those?"

Officer Nomura hesitated before saying, "The police force in River Heights is fairly small, and usually we're pretty much aware of each other's cases. But I'm afraid I don't remember anything about book thefts. Then again, it's not the kind of thing that we'd pay much attention to."

Nancy knew she couldn't give up so easily. "Maybe you didn't hear about the other thefts because they didn't happen in River Heights," she suggested. "What if they were in some neighboring town? Could you check with the nearby police departments?"

"If the chief okays it," Officer Nomura said reluctantly. "The truth is, Nancy, we're short-staffed. I don't know how much time I'll be allowed to give to a case like this one. I'm sorry I can't be more helpful right now."

"Well, then," Nancy said, "I may do some investigating on my own."

"I'm sure you will," Nomura said. "And let me know if you find out anything important."

As Nancy said goodbye and hung up the phone, Carson Drew gave her a questioning look. "I can almost see the wheels in your head spinning," he said. "What are you planning?"

Nancy laughed. "Well, first off," she said, "I'm going to ask George to set up a meeting for me with Lori Chang, so I can get some information about the rare book business. Then I want to check with those other police departments. If the River Heights police won't do it, I'll make the calls myself."

"Anything else?" her father asked.

Nancy smiled, enjoying the thrill of cracking open a new case. "I'd love to get some information on this Risa woman. Maybe tomorrow I can—"

"I thought you were going up to Emerson to see Ned tomorrow," Hannah broke in.

"Oh, right," Nancy said, feeling a bit embarrassed. She'd gotten so carried away with the case that she'd totally forgotten she was supposed to spend the next day at Emerson College with her boyfriend, Ned Nickerson.

"Should I call Ned and tell him you're too busy to see him?" her father teased her.

"No way," Nancy said. "I'll ask George to investigate Risa. Tomorrow I'll be at Emerson with Ned—that just means I'll get started Thursday!"

On Wednesday morning Nancy drove to Emerson College, where Ned was taking summer classes. She was determined to push her new case to the back of her mind and enjoy her visit with her boyfriend. But soon after they met, as they walked arm in arm across the green campus, Ned glanced at her and said, "Okay, Nan, I know that look in your eyes. You're on a new case, aren't you? Time to fill me in."

Nancy laughed. "Do you really want to hear about it?"

"Try me," he said.

Nancy eagerly told Ned about the mystery of the book thefts, starting with her visit to the rare book room. Neither the police nor her father were taking the thefts seriously, and she half-expected Ned to do the same. But his face grew thoughtful as he listened to her.

"Guess what?" he said when Nancy had finished. "There's been a rash of book thefts here at Emerson, too."

Nancy's eyebrows shot up in surprise. "Really? How do you know?" she asked.

"My friend David Desantos is a student security guard over at the library," Ned said. "He told me he's been trying to figure it out for weeks. Do you want to go talk to him?"

Nancy nodded eagerly. "You bet!"

The library, a modern building of reflective glass, was not far away. Luckily, David Desantos was on duty, stationed at the security checkpoint beside the library doors. When Ned introduced him to Nancy, David's eyes lit up.

"I was going to ask Ned to introduce me to you," he said. "I've heard about all the cases you've solved. Well, we've got a mystery for you here, all right."

David glanced around and lowered his voice. "We've had three rare editions stolen in the last six months," he went on. "No one knows who did it or how. You should meet our rare books curator, Gwen Buller. She'll tell you all about it."

On the second floor of the library Nancy and Ned found the curator, a brisk English woman with auburn hair swept back from a thin, intelligent-looking face. Gwen Buller confirmed what David had told them about the recent thefts. "The first two books to disappear were rare examples of early American printing techniques," she said. "One of them was printed by Benjamin Franklin. The third missing book is a first edition of *Gone with the Wind.*"

"Why do you think those particular books were taken?" Nancy asked the curator.

"For the money," Ms. Buller said promptly. "A

17

collector would pay several thousand dollars for any one of the stolen books."

"But couldn't the thief be a collector who wanted the books for his own library and didn't intend to sell them?" Nancy suggested.

Gwen shook her head. "That might be true if they'd all been on one topic or even related topics," she said. "Collectors usually specialize in a specific type of book. But it looks to me as though the thief just grabbed whatever he or she could get."

"Do the police have any leads?" Ned asked.

Ms. Buller sighed. "I'm afraid the police aren't spending much time investigating this case," she said. "To be fair, it probably doesn't seem quite as urgent to them as it is to us. But the most dreadful thing is that the police assume it may have been someone on staff."

"An inside job, you mean?" Nancy asked.

The curator nodded. "It's true that the librarians are the only ones with free access to the rare book room," she admitted. "But I can't believe someone on my staff would ever steal a book. We're in this field because we have great respect for books. Still . . ." She paused, and an uneasy expression crossed her face. "I can't help but look around now and wonder," she confessed. "I'd hate to think it's someone who works here. So I certainly hope you can solve our case for us, Nancy. We've all been on edge here ever since the thefts began."

"I'll do my best," Nancy promised the curator.

"Tell me, what sort of security system does the library use?"

"Like many libraries, we place little magnetic 'elements' between a book's inside spine and the outer cloth that covers it," Ms. Buller explained. "Everyone who leaves the library has to pass through an electronic gate down by the front doors. The gate 'announces' whenever a magnetized book passes through. Then the guard checks whether it's been properly signed out. If it's labeled a rare book, it's not supposed to leave the library at all."

"So every book in this library has been magnetized?" Nancy asked.

Gwen Buller gave a soft laugh. "I wish. We can't afford to magnetize every book we own, not even all the rare books. So instead we put the elements in a certain percentage of the books. It's usually enough to catch thieves."

"But it is possible for a thief to walk out with an unmagnetized book," Nancy said thoughtfully.

The curator nodded. "Also, I've heard that some thieves remove the magnetic element with a razor," she said in a voice edged with disapproval.

"May I see the room the books were stolen from?" Nancy asked.

Ms. Buller led Ned and Nancy down a hallway and through a set of glass doors into the rare book room, tucked away in the core of the library. Inside were book-lined walls and two long tables, where several students sat quietly working.

In a hushed voice, the curator explained that

19

visitors had to be personally let into the room by one of the rare book room's staff. No other books, bags, or purses were permitted. Visitors had to show a college ID, then sign in and sign out in a log book by the door. The door was always locked when the library was closed. Ms. Buller kept the key in her desk during the day and gave it to a security guard at night.

Nancy looked curiously around the small, brightly lit room. There were no dark corners, no place for a thief to hide while he or she slipped a book down a shirt or into a coat pocket. A staff member sat on a stool by the door, observing everyone.

Nancy looked at the students using the room. One young woman caught her eye. She looked oddly out of place, with her bright red hair chopped into a spiky haircut. She wore a torn T-shirt, black leather pants, and heavy black motorcycle boots.

Her spiky head bent over, the girl sat at the table, reading a slim white volume. Every few seconds she'd glance around nervously, as if afraid someone was watching her.

Nancy turned back to Ms. Buller. "I'd like to get a copy of your sign-in log for the last six months," she said, "to see if there are any suspicious visitation patterns. And I'd like to talk to your staff as well."

"I'll make the arrangements," the curator said. "We'll take the log and make a copy right now."

Ms. Buller turned to leave the room. Ned leapt

forward to open the door for her, and Nancy followed them.

As she did so, the red-haired girl suddenly grabbed her leather jacket and slipped in front of Nancy, edging through the door in front of Ms. Buller. Nancy realized that the girl hadn't stopped at the desk to sign out.

Then Nancy's blue eyes widened. Beneath the jacket on the girl's arm, she spied the corner of a slim white book.

"Hey!" Nancy cried. "Stop that girl!"

3

An Unexpected Threat

Nancy ran after the red-haired girl and grabbed her wrist. As the girl spun around, the book fell from under her arm, dropping to the floor.

"Look!" Nancy said, pointing to the book. "She took that out of the rare book room." Ned and Ms. Buller were immediately by Nancy's side.

"Are you calling me a thief?" the girl asked angrily.

"I saw you take that book," Nancy stated calmly.

"Just doing my job," the girl snapped, bending down to retrieve the book from the floor. "This book needs rebinding." She swiftly inspected the spine for damage.

"It's all right, Nancy," Ms. Buller said hurriedly. "This is Arianne Stone—she works here. Arianne, this is Nancy Drew. We've asked her to look into our book thefts."

Nancy felt her face flush with embarrassment.

"I'm really very sorry for the mistake," she apologized. "I don't usually leap to—"

But Arianne wasn't interested in her apology. "I'd like to get back to work now," she told Ms. Buller, pointedly ignoring Nancy.

The curator nodded, and the young woman left.

"Why don't you come to my office, Nancy," Ms. Buller said tactfully. "You might as well interview everyone on staff. I can send them to you there."

As they walked down the hall, the curator added in a low voice, "Arianne Stone is a library science student who works here part-time. She's a brilliant girl and knows a lot about old books, even though she doesn't look like your typical librarian. But I have to admit I've had my doubts about her."

"Regarding these thefts?" Nancy asked.

The curator nodded reluctantly. "Two of the books were stolen while she was on duty in the rare book room," she explained. "At the time of the third theft, Arianne claims she was out alone all night on her motorcycle. I've been keeping an eye on her."

Nancy made a mental note of this as she followed the curator into her small, book-crammed office. Ms. Buller seated Nancy at her desk and went out to call in staff members one by one.

After interviewing everyone on the rare book staff, Nancy's next stop was the campus security office. But as David and Ms. Buller had warned her, the officers there were no more helpful than the River Heights police had been. The chief said he had reported the thefts to the Emersonville police, but when Nancy checked with the police department, she was told that "missing library books are not a priority here."

That evening as Nancy and Ned sat together in the dining hall eating submarine sandwiches, Nancy pondered the case out loud. "What if these are just random thefts?" she asked Ned. "If there's no connection, there's no case."

Ned put his hand on hers. "If all your instincts are telling you there's a case, then I believe there is one," he said.

Nancy smiled at him, grateful for his support. "I'm going to get to the bottom of this," she declared. "And when I do, I bet we'll find my Sherlock Holmes book, too."

On Thursday morning, just after ten, Nancy met Bess in front of Bloom's Bookstore. George had set up a meeting with Lori Chang for eleven, and the three friends planned to have coffee at Bloom's before setting out for the bookbinder's shop.

"Where's George?" Nancy asked.

"She'll be about fifteen minutes late," Bess explained. "She had an aerobics class that she forgot about when she said she'd meet us." Bess glanced in through the bookstore window. "Do you think Richard's here today?" she asked as she fidgeted with the barrette in her hair.

"Let's find out," Nancy said.

They entered the bookstore. It was quieter than it had been the night of the reading, but the shop still had the same warm, welcoming feel. Bess anxiously scanned the store. "I don't see him anywhere," she said to Nancy, "I'll ask around."

A young man behind the coffee bar pointed Bess to Cyril Bloom's office, behind a door marked Bank Manager.

Nancy and Bess found Cyril sitting behind a large antique desk, typing rapidly on a computer keyboard. He paused when he saw the two girls at the door. "Good morning," he said. "Can I help you find anything?"

"Richard Munro?" Bess said hopefully.

Cyril smiled. "I'm afraid Richard won't be in today," he said. "He's preparing for a reading he'll be giving at my house tomorrow night."

"Oh," Bess said, disappointment in her voice. "I wrote a poem yesterday, and was hoping to show it to him. I'm Bess Marvin, and this is my friend Nancy Drew."

"Oh, yes. I remember you from the other night," he said to Nancy. "You were interested in the rare book room." Then he gave Bess a sympathetic glance. "Would you two like to come to the poetry reading?"

"I'd love to," Bess said with a smile.

"That would be great," Nancy added. A poetry reading would be just the place to find out more about the rare book world, she thought. "Actually," she said to Cyril, "I wonder if I could ask you a few questions about rare books."

"Go right ahead," Cyril said, leaning back in his chair. "Are you a collector?"

"No, Nancy's a detective," Bess answered.

"She's solved dozens of cases. Sometimes I help, too."

Nancy winced, wishing Bess hadn't said that. Working on a case was always easier if no one knew who she was. Still, it couldn't be undone now. She saw Cyril sit up, raising his eyebrows in interest. "I was visiting a friend at Emerson College yesterday," she explained. "He told me that the library there has had several rare books stolen. And I've heard that rare books in this area have disappeared, also. Do you know anything about the thefts?"

Cyril rubbed his chin thoughtfully. "I don't know anything about Emerson's problems," he said. "I'm never in that area. But yes, there have been a few thefts around here recently."

"Could they be connected?" Nancy asked.

Cyril shook his head. "I doubt it," he said. "Rare books are often very valuable and relatively easy to steal. I can't tell you how many collectors are sloppy about security. Even I had one stolen, and I've got a computerized security system."

"Someone broke through your system?" Nancy asked.

"Actually, no," Cyril replied. "I can't blame the system. The book was taken from my car—I forgot to lock it. I never even got the book into the store." He gave her a rueful smile.

Bess peered at Cyril's computer screen. "Hey, you have the same computer as my dad," she said. "He's really hooked on it. Every night he's busy sending electronic mail to all his friends."

"I'm an e-mail freak myself," Cyril admitted, turning from Nancy to Bess. "It's a great way to communicate." As he watched Bess stare at the screen, Cyril's eyes lit up. "You know, Richard is on-line, too," he told her. "If I give you his computer address, you could send him that poem."

"Really?" Bess asked enthusiastically.

"Really," Cyril said. He wrote down the name of a computer network, followed by a series of numbers. "Your dad can show you how to get into the network," he explained, handing the paper to Bess. "Then you just send your poem to this number. Be sure to type in your network address, too. That way, Richard can write back to you."

"Wow," Bess murmured.

Cyril smiled and handed Bess an ivory envelope. "And here's the invitation to the reading," he said.

Nancy glanced at her watch. "George is probably wondering where we are," she reminded Bess. "Thanks for all the help, Mr. Bloom."

"Any time," he replied.

Nancy and Bess spotted George waiting at the coffee bar when they left Cyril's office. "Where have you two been?" she asked.

"Getting information," Nancy said. At the same time, Bess said, "Getting invited to Richard Munro's poetry reading."

George looked at her two friends and laughed. "Sounds like we're definitely headed for trouble."

George grabbed a bagel and orange juice, and

the three friends piled into Nancy's Mustang to drive to the bookbinding workshop. The address Lori had given George was in Oakville, a town about twenty miles away. As they drove, Nancy told the girls about the Emerson book thefts. George, in turn, told what she had learned about Risa, the book collector.

"Risa Palmetto is the widow of a wealthy furniture manufacturer. She was his second wife," said George. "Apparently, the children of his first wife are furious that she's spending all their dad's money on expensive rare books. She's one of Cyril's best customers. She's known him for years."

"Maybe they were in love," Bess said dreamily. "I bet she married the other guy for his money, but it broke her heart to leave Cyril behind."

Nancy laughed, remembering how Risa had called Cyril a double-crossing toad the other day. "I think you're letting your imagination run wild, Bess. Let's stick to the facts," she said. "This is detective work, not poetry."

Lori's directions brought them to a plain white wooden farmhouse. Behind it was an old barn made of fieldstone and graying timber. "See the name on the mailbox?" George pointed out. "Leonard Sather—he's the man Lori works for. She told me that he and his wife live in the farmhouse. Lori lives in a studio apartment in the barn, above the workshop."

As Nancy parked the car by the barn, Lori

opened the workshop door. "Hi, guys. Come on in," she said.

Inside was a huge room filled with big wooden worktables. Two walls were covered with shelves of old books, while a third wall was hung with posters of book designs from museums around the world. The fourth wall had large windows over-looking green farmland. Overhead, a vast assort-ment of tools hung from hooks. Some looked familiar; the others were special bookbinding tools, Nancy guessed.

"How many of you work here?" Nancy asked Lori.

"Just me and Leonard," Lori answered. "It's really a one-person operation. I'm lucky a master craftsman like Leonard lets me work with him at all. He's gone into town, but maybe you'll meet him later. Anyway, let me show you around."

Books in various stages of construction crowded the tabletops. Lori showed the girls how the covers were made of board wrapped with cloth or leath-er, then the pages were sewed by hand into the binding. Fancy endpapers, with swirling marbled designs, were then put on the inside covers.

"Look at this," Bess marveled, running her finger along the cover of a book bound in navy blue leather stamped in gold. "It's as smooth as glove leather and twice as beautiful."

Lori smiled. "I never knew books could be such gorgeous objects before I started working here," she said. "Most books today are just glued together in factories. There aren't many bookbinders around like Leonard, who can give fine books a special binding."

"Look at this," George said, picking up a miniature edition of *Hamlet*. The book couldn't have been more than one inch square. It had a red leather binding, and gold-leaf decorated the edges of the pages. Inside were tiny woodcut illustrations, showing the prince of Denmark and Shakespeare's other characters. "Do people really read books this tiny?" George asked in amazement.

"Only with a magnifying glass," Lori replied. "Mostly they're for collectors."

After their tour, Nancy told Lori about her case. Lori listened, nodding. "Quite a few local collectors have had books stolen or missing lately," she said when Nancy was done. "It sure seems like too many thefts to be just a coincidence."

"I agree," Nancy said. "The curator at Emerson thinks the thief is stealing books to sell them."

"I don't agree with that," Lori said. "Risa and some of the other collectors who've been hit all had more valuable books that *weren't* stolen. It seems that this thief wanted specific titles, as if he or she were building a collection."

"If that were the case, the books would all have something in common, wouldn't they?" Nancy asked. "They would all be about the same subject or be by the same writer."

"Possibly," Lori said. "But there are many reasons why books are collected. It isn't just a question of who wrote it or what it's about. Some collectors gather examples of various printing methods or unusual binding styles or leather-stamped cover designs. Or maybe a collector is interested in the work of one master engraver. There are all sorts of things these stolen books might have in common."

"Hey, look at this!" Bess cried out. She was standing over a worktable where the pages of an old book were spread out, waiting to be sewed back together. Bess carefully picked up a clump of pages. "This book is by Cyril Bloom, and it looks like love poems," she said. "This poem is called 'The Dark Lady Passes.' Wow, it's really romantic."

Lori walked over to join Bess. "Leonard's putting beautiful new bindings on some of Cyril's books," she explained, "including the one he wrote. Leonard's found some absolutely gorgeous Moroccan leather for them and—"

At that moment the door opened. An older man with a strong, ruddy face and piercing blue eyes stood glowering in the doorway. "Put that down!" he barked.

Bess turned pale and quickly set the pages down. She started to apologize, but the man cut her off. "What is going on here?"

Bess and George began to move toward the door, but Nancy stood still. "Mr. Sather," she said firmly, "my name's Nancy Drew. I just came to ask Lori a few questions—"

"Get out of my workshop," he spat out. "I don't care who you are, and I don't want you in here."

"But Nancy is trying to find out what she can about the stolen books," Lori put in.

Sather's face went even redder, and his eyes darkened with anger. He grasped the door handle tightly and spat out, "Ms. Drew, I want you out of here this instant!"

4

A Mysterious Message

Without another word, Nancy marched out of the bookbindery with George and Bess. Lori ran out after them, making sure the shop door was closed so Sather couldn't hear. "I'm so sorry," she said. "It's all my fault. I know Leonard doesn't like people in the workshop. I just wasn't expecting him back so soon."

"It's all right," Nancy said. "When he calms down, tell him we're sorry we upset him."

Bess looked over her shoulder at the workshop door. "He doesn't seem like a very nice man to work for," she said.

"Leonard? Oh, you just have to get to know him," Lori replied. "He's a loner—he's not very good with people. He's much better with books."

The girls said goodbye to Lori and got back in Nancy's car. "We're not much closer to solving the book thefts, are we?" Bess asked as they drove off.

Nancy sighed. "Not a bit."

On Friday evening Nancy and George stopped at the Marvins' house to pick up Bess for Richard Munro's poetry reading. Bess came out the front door wearing a long, flowered summer dress. A frilly pink bow pulled back her blond hair.

After climbing into the car, Bess opened her purse and took out a sheaf of papers. "What is all that?" Nancy asked as she pulled away from the curb.

"My poetry," Bess announced. "Ever since Cyril gave me Richard's e-mail address yesterday, I've been writing like mad. I send Richard my poems as soon as they're done. Richard says I've got tremendous talent. He says my poems are wonderful."

"He does?" George asked.

"Of course," Bess said. "This"—she waved the sheaf of poems at them—"is the start of one of the world's great romantic correspondences."

"Has Richard sent you poems, too?" Nancy asked.

"Not yet," Bess admitted. "But he's been too busy getting ready for the reading and everything."

"So read us one of yours," George said, trading a skeptical glance with Nancy.

"Well, this one's called 'The Beginning,'" Bess announced. She cleared her throat and read:

"Oh, my dear sweetheart
When we are apart
I want you near
My sweetheart my dear.
So let us start
and eat an apple tart.
Today our love begins.

"What do you think?" Bess asked.

There was silence in the car. Both Nancy and George tried to think of something to say. At last Nancy said, "It's very . . . you."

"It is, isn't it?" Bess said, sounding pleased. "It's about my favorite things—food and romance. Richard says you have to write about what really matters to you. Otherwise the poems are hollow and false. Especially love poems."

"So you've been reading a lot of love poems lately?" Nancy asked, hiding a smile.

"I spent hours at the library today," Bess admitted. "And guess what? I found that book of Cyril's, *The Dark Lady*. It's so dreamy—all these poems he wrote to an unnamed woman."

"I wonder who she was," George said curiously.

"I think it was Risa Palmetto," Bess said. "I bet Cyril broke her heart when she was young. Or maybe she turned *him* down because he was a starving young poet and she was determined to be rich."

"Bess," Nancy said, laughing, "we know almost nothing about this woman. Don't you think you

35

ought to have a few more facts before jumping to a conclusion like that?"

"I am *not* jumping to conclusions," Bess said indignantly. "I'm just using my intuition. You know, Nan, you're not the only detective around here. I'll get the real story on Cyril and Risa. You conduct your investigation, and I'll conduct mine. Just call me the Love Detective!"

A few minutes later, they pulled up at Cyril Bloom's house, a beautiful modern building of wood and glass surrounded by tall beech trees. The circular driveway was crowded with cars. Bess pointed to a red sports car parked beside a battered motorcycle. "That must be Richard's car," she said, excited. "The license plate says **THE BARD**. That's how he signs his letters to me."

"Nice car," George commented. "I didn't realize there was so much money to be made in poetry."

"Actually I don't think there is," Nancy said, perplexed. She remembered Lori Chang's comment about Richard's expensive tastes. Where did Richard's money come from? she wondered.

Inside, the house was stark and modern—the total opposite of the cozy clutter at Bloom's Bookstore. The furniture was mostly black, each chair and table standing out dramatically against the white walls. The guests were gathered in the living room, a high-ceilinged room with glass walls looking out into the trees.

Nancy was surprised to see what a large crowd had come to hear Richard read. She immediately spotted Risa, wearing another extravagant hat— this one had dried flowers and a bird made of real feathers sitting on the brim. If her hat didn't draw enough attention to her, her voice definitely did. She was talking so loudly that she could be heard above the crowd. Then, as she scanned the room, Nancy's eyes lit on a head of spiky red hair. "Arianne Stone," she gasped softly in surprise.

George followed Nancy's gaze. "What's she doing here? It's a long way from Emerson," George said.

"Maybe she rode here on that old motorcycle outside," Nancy said. "Gwen Buller told me that Arianne has a motorcycle." She turned to face her friends. "Hey, where's Bess?"

"Guess," George said, pointing to a circle of women surrounding Richard Munro. Bess sat on the outer edge, smiling happily. From what Nancy could tell, Richard wasn't even aware that Bess was there. He was talking intently to a tanned young woman who looked like a model.

At the other end of the room, Nancy saw Cyril Bloom standing beside a long table. On it lay several copies of Richard's new book, *A Question of the Heart*. Nancy nodded to George, and they started toward the table. But halfway across the room, they suddenly ran into Lori Chang with Leonard Sather.

When Sather saw Nancy, he scowled and turned

37

away, elbowing his way through the crowd to the door. Lori shrugged as she watched him go. "That's my boss, Mr. Personality," she joked. Nancy smiled, but as she watched him go, she thought, Either Leonard Sather is one of the rudest men I've ever met, or he's a man with something to hide.

"Is Mr. Sather a poetry fan?" George asked.

"Actually he is," Lori said. "He's one of the best-read people you'll ever meet. But the real reason Leonard drags himself to these gatherings is that it's good for business. Cyril has referred a lot of customers to Leonard."

"Does he need to drum up business?" Nancy asked. "Your workshop seemed plenty busy to me."

"Oh, it is," said Lori. "But he's always worried about money, with his wife and all—" Lori stopped and flushed.

"What about his wife?" Nancy prompted her.

"I guess it's not really a secret," Lori said. "But Leonard doesn't talk about it much himself. His wife has a rare bone disease. She used to be able to get around in a wheelchair, but now she can't even get out of bed. It's been hard for them these last few years, and expensive, too. All those medical bills sometimes make him feel kind of desperate."

Desperate enough to steal books? Nancy wondered. Books valuable enough to sell for cash but not so valuable that the police would take interest? Sather knew the book field; he knew who had

38

what, who was selling and who was buying. In spite of Lori's faith in her boss, Nancy decided to keep her eye on Sather. She felt sympathy for his wife, but the man himself she didn't trust.

"By the way," Lori went on, "one of the local collectors who's had books stolen is here tonight —Risa Palmetto, that short woman in the hat. Want me to introduce you?"

"Yes, please," Nancy said. They made their way over to the corner of the room, where Risa was chattering away to an elderly man. He slipped away when Lori tapped Risa's shoulder.

"Hello, dear," Risa said, kissing Lori's cheek. "How's the repair job going on my new book?"

"We're almost done," Lori assured her. "Risa, I'd like you to meet my friends George Fayne and Nancy Drew. Nancy is investigating the recent book thefts in the area. She'd like to speak to you about your stolen books."

Nancy wished Lori hadn't told Risa she was investigating, but maybe Risa would be willing to answer some questions now that she knew.

"Oh, don't remind me of the stolen books!" Risa said, dramatically putting her hand to her forehead, or as close as her large hat would allow. "It was ghastly, knowing someone had actually been in my house. Oh, good heavens, there's Martin. Martin, over here!"

"I'd like to ask you a few questions about the theft, if I may," Nancy said.

"Not now, dear, I really must speak to Martin,"

the little woman said, brushing Nancy aside. She bustled after a thick-set man who had just come through the door.

Did Risa run off because she didn't want to answer my questions? Nancy wondered. This case is full of people who are trying to avoid me, she thought with a sigh.

"I'll try her again later," Nancy said aloud. "But it doesn't look like Risa's going to be easy to pin down."

"You can probably catch her at the Rendell's auction tomorrow," Lori suggested. "Rendell's is an auction house that specializes in antiques. They have a rare book auction once a month, and tomorrow is the day. I know because Leonard always goes. I'll give you all the details."

The poetry reading was about to start, so Nancy, Lori, and George settled on the floor to listen. Nancy noticed that Bess had found herself a seat only an arm's length away from Richard. He really was quite talented, Nancy had to admit. She enjoyed his poems so much that afterward she stood in line to buy a copy of his book and have it signed. Arianne was also in line, and when Nancy looked at her to say hello, the red-haired student quickly glanced away.

"It's great of you to go to all this trouble for Richard," Nancy said to Cyril as she paid him for the book.

"Well, I feel it's the duty of us old-timers to help the younger generation of artists get started," the silver-haired poet told her proudly. "That's why I set up poetry readings and hang young painters' canvases at the shop."

Nancy smiled at the handsome older man. "I'd hardly describe you as an old-timer," she said.

Cyril shook his head. "Like my books, I belong to the past," he said. "But that's all right. The past is filled with many beautiful things."

Nancy handed Richard the book to sign. Bess was standing between Richard and Cyril, looking like she was having the time of her life. Nancy hated to have to end her evening. "I'm afraid we have to go," Nancy told Bess. "I just told George I'd find you and meet her at the car."

"Already?" Bess said. "Oh, well, all right. But first I want you to take a picture for me." She fished a small camera out of her bag and handed it to Nancy. "Richard, can you just move over this way a minute? Nancy's going to take our picture."

Nancy put down her purse and book and followed Bess and Richard to a spot near the windows. Richard posed with his arm around Bess and a very photogenic smile on his face. He seemed to enjoy having his picture taken. Nancy quickly snapped a shot, then handed the camera back to Bess. "I'll get my things," Nancy murmured, leaving her friend to say good night to the poet.

As Nancy picked up her book and purse, she looked over and saw Richard give Bess a dazzling smile, the same smile Nancy had seen him use on half a dozen girls that evening. When Bess left, he started up a conversation with a very attractive woman in red, who seemed to enjoy the attention

41

he was giving her. Bess practically floated over to join Nancy.

George was waiting for them at the car. "So, Bess, was it a night to remember?" she asked her cousin.

"Oh, yes," Bess said with a contented sigh. "It's all just too romantic, isn't it?"

"Yes, it is," said Nancy under her breath. She was beginning to worry about her friend.

Nancy was on her way up to bed that night when she realized that she'd never gotten a chance to read what Richard had written in her book. He had probably just signed his name, she told herself. Still, she was curious.

She picked up her tote bag and took out the book. It was a beautiful slim volume, bound in fine green linen with the title *A Question of the Heart* printed in curving black script.

Nancy opened the book to the front page. Beneath the title the poet had written: "Best wishes to Nancy from Richard Munro."

But then Nancy gasped. Beneath Richard's signature, someone had added another message in a very different handwriting: "If you value your life, Nancy Drew, stop asking questions!"

5

The Book Thief Strikes Again

Curious, Nancy examined the threatening message someone had written to her in Richard Munro's book of poems. It was in brown ink in a beautiful old-fashioned script. It didn't look like anyone's day-to-day handwriting; it was formal and decorative, like something from an old manuscript.

Who would have done this? she wondered. Several people at Cyril's that night knew she was investigating the book thefts: Lori, Leonard Sather, Arianne Stone, Risa Palmetto, Cyril himself. And anyone else in the room might have easily overheard her talking to Lori or Risa.

Nancy glanced down at the handwritten message again. This must have been done when I put the book down to take Richard and Bess's picture, she thought. The message was written with a fountain pen, and whoever did it had made a special effort to disguise his or her normal handwriting by writing in a fancy style. "That's so I can't trace the handwriting to someone," Nancy murmured to herself. "Very clever."

So who was the mystery man or woman who wanted her to stop investigating? Nancy wondered. And what would that person do if she didn't stop?

Just then Hannah poked her head in the door to say good night. Nancy showed her the message written in the book. "I must be on the right trail," Nancy said. "Why else would someone be trying to warn me off?"

Hannah eyed the message warily. "Maybe you should let the police know about this," she said.

"I will," Nancy promised, "as soon as I have more facts. Something that proves that I'm right and that all these book thefts are connected."

Hannah sighed. "Where do you look for proof like that?" she asked.

"Tomorrow I'll go to the local libraries and find out if they've had any thefts recently," Nancy said. "George has a tennis match, and Bess is busy writing poetry, so I'm on my own. I can also check with some neighboring police departments. Then in the afternoon, there's a rare book auction I want to go to."

"An auction?" Hannah said. "I adore auctions, though I've never been to one for books. May I come along?"

"Of course, I'd love the company," Nancy said happily. "I'll give you the details in the morning."

* * *

Nancy had a busy Saturday morning. First she phoned the police stations in the neighboring towns. No one had reports on a book thief. Then she drove from library to library in the area. Around noon she headed over to Rendell's Auction House, which was north of town. When she pulled her blue Mustang into the parking lot, Hannah was outside waiting for her. She had driven herself over in the Drews' family car.

"Did you learn anything at the libraries this morning?" Hannah asked as they crossed the crowded parking lot.

"Just as I thought, there have been several thefts in the last year," Nancy replied. "River Heights Community College lost a whole shelf from its late nineteenth-century collection. A whole shelf!"

"That's one bold thief," Hannah commented.

"And a skillful one, too," Nancy said.

They entered the building, stepping into a large white room, where many books has been put on display. The most expensive were in glass cases, while books of lesser value lay on a table in a smaller side room. Beyond the two preview rooms was the auction room itself.

A large crowd had already gathered to preview the books. Nancy spotted Risa Palmetto at once. She was hard to miss in her shiny purple jumpsuit and leopard-print pillbox hat. Through a glass door labeled Auction Office, she also saw Cyril Bloom and Richard Munro talking with members of Rendell's staff. Nancy pointed out the bookseller and his assistant to Hannah. Then she noticed a familiar dour face.

"See that man?" Nancy said to Hannah. "That's Lori's boss, Leonard Sather. I don't trust him. He was at Cyril's house last night so he could have written that message."

"Shall I try to follow him around?" Hannah asked. "He knows you, but he won't recognize me."

Nancy nodded. "That's a good idea. I'm going to talk to Risa." She edged through the crowd toward the collector. But Risa, seeing Nancy, turned immediately to walk off toward the auction office.

Nancy frowned and turned back to the books on display. Hannah and Leonard Sather were right in front of her. She heard Hannah innocently ask the bookbinder if he was planning to bid on anything today.

Sather growled, "I've just come to look at these manuscripts. I'm not a buyer—these are way out of my league." Then his voice softened and grew almost wistful. "But aren't they the most beautiful things you've ever seen?"

The manuscripts he was talking about lay under glass in their own special case. The way they were displayed gave Nancy the impression that they were the most valuable items in the auction.

"Magnificent, aren't they?" said a gentle voice over Nancy's shoulder. She looked up at a tall, attractive man with dark hair.

"They come from a fourteenth-century monastery," the man explained. "Each one is an entire book written out by hand. Just imagine holding something so old in your own hands!"

Nancy looked at the gorgeous little paintings of knights and their ladies that decorated the manuscripts' pages. The bright blues and reds and golds made the tiny scenes so real, she almost expected to hear the horses whinny and the trumpets sound. "It's amazing," she agreed. "I feel as if I could step right into the Middle Ages."

The man smiled at her, his eyes bright with enthusiasm. "I'm William Laws," he introduced himself, handing her his card. "I'm a book dealer. My wife and I run a mail-order company called Truepenny Books."

Nancy told him her name but not that she was investigating the stolen books. There was something about William Laws's face that made him seem trustworthy, but she hesitated to tell him all about her case. She decided to tell him instead that she was interested in becoming a collector. "I'd like to learn all I can about the rare book business," she explained.

"I'll gladly tell you what I know," Laws offered.

"Because these books are so valuable," Nancy began, "they might get stolen. But who would thieves try to sell stolen books to—a dealer? And would a dealer know that the books were 'hot'?"

"A dealer might be aware that a book had been stolen if he'd heard about it on the rare book grapevine," Laws said. "Or he might be able to tell by examining the book itself. Certain collectors have special marks of ownership that they put in their books. A knowledgeable book person could tell just who had owned that book by these marks. Let me show you."

He ushered Nancy into the smaller room where the books of lesser value were displayed on long tables. He picked up a volume at random: a London 1885 edition of Robert Louis Stevenson's *Treasure Island.*

"A bookplate is one of the most obvious marks of ownership," Laws explained. "This one tells us that the book once belonged to Skipper Marie, a famous nineteenth-century book collector. Because Marie is so well known, this mark of ownership actually increases the value of the book to a serious collector. But this bookplate is a fake—a copy someone made of Marie's plate, trying to raise this book's value."

"How can you tell it's a fake?" Nancy asked, fascinated.

"Simple. Marie collected in the 1860s. *Treasure Island* wasn't even published until the 1880s," Laws replied with a smile. Then, turning to the title page, he showed Nancy a tiny *XOX* lightly penciled in at the top of the page. "This is another ownership mark, from one of our local dealers," he said. "Collectors leave these marks intact. They're all part of the history of a book."

"A thief would try to get rid of these marks, wouldn't he?" Nancy commented.

Laws nodded. "Yes. But some marks of ownership are so subtle that a thief might not know where to find them. For instance, I have one client who circles the page number on page six of every book she owns."

"So if a book came to you that had an ownership mark you recognized," Nancy asked the book dealer, "would you call around before you bought it to make sure it hadn't been stolen?"

"Certainly, if I was buying from an unknown source," he replied. "So would all the collectors I do business with. But book people can be good or bad, like anyone else. There are unscrupulous collectors who won't hesitate to buy a book even if it's perfectly obvious it was stolen."

"So a thief *could* find a market for these stolen volumes," Nancy said.

"Yes," Laws said. He glanced at her intently. "Actually, I've heard of an unusual number of thefts in this area lately."

"Is that so?" Nancy said noncommitally. "Well, I hope the thief is caught soon."

"If you have any other questions," Mr. Laws offered, "you have my card. Please don't hesitate to call."

The crowd had begun to edge into the auction room. "I think the sale is about to start," Laws told Nancy. "Shall we go inside and get some good seats?"

"I should find the friend I came with," Nancy said. "I'll see you in there. Thanks for the information."

Nancy found Hannah bent over a glass case,

looking at a precious book. Opals, rubies, turquoise, and sapphires were set into the hand-tooled leather cover.

"Isn't it exquisite?" Hannah murmured.

"It sure is," Nancy agreed. "The auction's about to begin, so I'm going inside. Do you want to keep looking at the books out here?"

"Oh, I'll go with you," Hannah said. "I want to see what kind of person buys a book like this."

The seats in the auction room were nearly filled by the time Nancy and Hannah got inside. Nancy made her way to the back of the room. She could see Risa Palmetto sitting near the front of the room, near the podium where the auctioneer stood, a wooden gavel in his hand. Cyril Bloom sat in the middle of the room, several rows in front of Nancy, with Richard Munro beside him. William Laws was on the other side of the room, studying his catalog.

At the very back of the room, Nancy found two empty chairs. As she and Hannah sat down, Nancy spied another familiar face a few rows up, beneath a thatch of spiky red hair. Arianne Stone was there, too!

At the podium the auctioneer pounded his gavel and the auction began. Nancy was amazed at how quickly the bidding went. The auctioneer spoke so fast, she could barely follow the sale of the first few books. But once she got used to the rapid way he chanted the bids, the auction became much easier to understand.

"Item number seven," the auctioneer called out.

"A first printing of Samuel Johnson's *Dictionary.*" A man to his left held up the dictionary, then placed it on a display stand. "Do I have five thousand? Fifty-five hundred? Six thousand? Six-five, do I have six thousand five hundred dollars?"

"Who's bidding?" Hannah whispered to Nancy. "I don't hear anyone calling out."

"See that man near the front of the room wearing the red shirt?" Nancy said. "He just raised his finger. I think that was a bid."

"Six-five," the auctioneer went on. He looked at someone else in the audience, who nodded. That brought the price up to seven thousand dollars.

"Better not nod your head," Hannah murmured, "or you might end up owning some very expensive books."

Seconds later the sale was concluded at seven thousand dollars, and the auctioneer started on the next book in the catalog.

Nancy glanced down at her catalog for a second to read the description of the book being auctioned. When she looked up again, she saw Cyril leaning against the wall not far away. He raised one finger and bought a book for four hundred dollars.

"Item nine," the auctioneer called out, the first illustrated English edition of Stevenson's *Treasure Island.* Do I have fifty dollars? Seventy-five?"

"That's going cheap," Hannah remarked. "I was beginning to think you couldn't buy a book here without spending five hundred dollars."

"Look," Nancy said. "Cyril's bidding, and so is

Risa, and so is someone over toward the left." Nancy couldn't quite make out the third bidder, but Risa was easy to spot, waving her arm wildly at the auctioneer.

"One hundred thirty-five dollars," the auctioneer said. "Do I have one fifty?"

Cyril bid, but when the auctioneer asked for one seventy-five, Cyril dropped out, and the book went to the third bidder.

Risa stood up and stormed over to Cyril as the auctioneer began to sell the next item. "Cyril Bloom, how dare you bid against me?" Risa exploded loudly. "You knew perfectly well that I wanted that book!"

Cyril shrugged. "I was bidding for another client who was willing to spend more," he said. "Besides, neither one of us got it."

"Well, you should have been bidding for *me*," Risa said indignantly.

"Madam," the auctioneer said to Risa from the podium, "please lower your voice. You're disrupting the auction."

"There's no point in my staying," Risa replied bitterly. "I didn't get what I wanted, anyway." Then she jammed her hat on her head and stormed out of the room. Cyril trailed after, an apologetic look on his face. Nancy noticed Richard Munro following his boss out of the room.

The auction resumed, and once again Nancy found herself fascinated by the play of collectors and dealers buying beautiful books for enormous sums. Arianne watched as intently as Nancy, but like many of the onlookers, she didn't bid.

The next item was the group of fourteenth-century manuscripts Nancy had been looking at with William Laws. A ripple of excitement went through the room when they were sold to Laws for thirteen thousand dollars. "I want to congratulate Mr. Laws," Nancy told Hannah as the auction ended. "I'll only be a minute."

But as she got up to walk toward the book dealer, another voice rose over the murmurings of the crowd. "Will everyone please remain exactly where they are?"

A startled silence fell over the crowd. Everyone turned to see a police officer barring the door.

With a grim face, he announced, "The *Alice in Wonderland* book, a first edition illustrated by Arthur Rackham, has been stolen!"

6

Things Get Serious

Nancy scanned the crowd as police officers swarmed into the auction room. She looked to see what Arianne Stone's reaction to all this would be. But Arianne wasn't in the room!

"How could someone as striking as Arianne slip out without my noticing?" Nancy said to Hannah.

"Maybe she left when we were distracted by the argument between that loud little woman and your bookseller friend," Hannah suggested.

Biting her lip in frustration, Nancy looked around the room. "And where's Leonard Sather?" she asked uneasily.

"You know, I don't think he ever came into the auction," Hannah told Nancy. "He told me he just came to look at the books in the preview room. I think he left before the bidding began."

"Everyone please take a seat," called out a middle-aged officer who looked familiar to Nancy.

She and Hannah sat down as the officer introduced himself as Lieutenant Walker.

"We've had a theft here," he said, "and we're going to be asking everyone some questions. So please be patient. You may be here awhile." He squinted in Nancy's direction and a second later was walking toward her.

"Nancy Drew," he said, reaching out to shake her hand. "I didn't expect to find you here. But then, I didn't expect anyone to steal from Rendell's. This is the first time they've had a theft."

"Quite a number of rare books have disappeared in this area lately," Nancy told the lieutenant. "I've been working on the case. If it's okay with you, I'd like to talk to the management here and see if there's a connection to the other stolen books."

"Go right ahead," Lieutenant Walker said. "My officers are questioning everyone in the audience now. You're welcome to go over our notes if you'll let me in on what you've found."

"I don't have much so far," Nancy admitted. "But there were five people who came to the auction and didn't stay to the end." Then Nancy told the lieutenant what she knew about Leonard Sather, Risa Palmetto, Arianne Stone, Cyril Bloom, and Richard Munro. "They may not be suspects," she finished, "but it's interesting that they all left before the theft was discovered."

"We'll check them out," Lieutenant Walker

promised. "Let me introduce you to Mr. Rendell, the man who owns the auction house."

Nancy told Hannah she'd be back in a few minutes, then she followed the lieutenant to Mr. Rendell's office.

Mr. Rendell was a burly man with black hair and a black mustache. He sat in a tiny office, talking on the phone. "Yes, of course, it was insured," he was saying in an agitated voice. "Everything here is insured. No, I don't know when we'll get it back. We're doing the best we can!" He hung up the phone and gave Lieutenant Walker a weary look. "The owner of the book is not pleased."

"I'm not surprised," Lieutenant Walker said. "Mr. Rendell, this is Nancy Drew. Nancy's a detective who's worked with us on a number of cases. She'd like to ask you a few questions."

Rendell waved to a wooden chair on the other side of the desk. "Have a seat, Ms. Drew."

Nancy told Rendell about the other stolen books, then asked him to tell her about the book that had just disappeared from the auction house.

"It was *Alice's Adventures in Wonderland,* illustrated by Arthur Rackham," Mr. Rendell explained. "Not terribly old, mind you, but it was valuable because of the illustrations. We estimated the price should be about six hundred dollars."

"Was this book on display in one of the glass cases or in the smaller preview room?" Nancy asked.

"In the smaller room," Mr. Rendell answered.

"It was hardly the most expensive item in the auction," Nancy said. "A thief could have taken more valuable books here today. This seems to be the work of someone who wanted that specific title. Can you think of anyone in the book collecting world who might have a particular interest in that book?"

Mr. Rendell was silent for a moment, then said, "I can think of about twenty people. Shall I write up a list for you?"

"Please," Nancy said. "Meanwhile, I'd like to look around the preview room again."

"Be my guest," Mr. Rendell told her.

In the preview room Nancy found Officer Nomura examining the glass display cases. "Nancy," she said, "it looks like you were right. There's definitely a string of book thefts going on."

"So why are the police suddenly so excited about this one?" Nancy joked.

"I'm sorry I didn't take your earlier report more seriously," Officer Nomura apologized. "But I did do some checking around after you called, and I have a list of local book thefts." The officer opened a notebook she was carrying and showed the list to Nancy. "I'll make you a copy," she promised.

Nancy quickly glanced at the list of victims. She saw Risa's and Cyril's names, along with five others she didn't recognize. "Were any of these thefts similar to the one at Rendell's?" she asked the officer.

"Not really," Nomura replied. "Rendell's has an

excellent security system. We're all amazed that someone cracked it. These display cases, for example, are protected by infrared light. If anyone opens them or moves them without deactivating the system, an alarm goes off right at the police station."

"But there are only a few items in these special cases," Nancy pointed out. "What about the rest of the books?"

"Good question," Lieutenant Walker said, joining them. "I already talked to Mr. Rendell about that. The less valuable items are kept in the small preview room, with a guard watching over them during the preview. All of those books were accounted for when the auction began, including the *Alice in Wonderland.* When the auction started, half the books were taken to the auction block and the door was locked. Later on the second half, with the *Alice in Wonderland* book, would have been taken out. And there should have been a guard near the door through the auction. I just don't understand how this could have happened."

"Who had the key to the door?" Nancy asked.

"There's no key," the lieutenant explained. He showed her an electronic keypad outside the door leading into the room. "You have to punch in the letters of a special password here. Only members of Rendell's staff know the password, which leads us to suspect that this is an in-house job. That's why Mr. Rendell is so upset."

Just like at the Emerson library, Nancy thought. The curator there, Gwen Buller, was also worried that her library thefts were inside jobs. It seemed to Nancy that the two cases were connected.

"Was anything else missing from the locked room?" she asked.

"Nothing," the lieutenant answered. "We're dusting it for prints now."

Nancy noticed that people were filing out of the auction room. "I think my officers have finished their questioning," Lieutenant Walker said. "Why don't you stop by the station later this week, Nancy, and you can go through the reports?"

"I will," Nancy said. "Thank you." She said goodbye to the police officers, then went to find Hannah.

Still sitting in the back row of seats, Hannah was the only person left in the room. She looked extremely cross.

"Hannah, what's wrong?" Nancy asked. "I'm sorry if I took so long. I—"

"It's not you I'm mad at," Hannah said. "It's those police. They know you and your dad, and they know I've been working for you for years. And yet they questioned me as if I was a criminal!"

"The police were just trying to get as much information as they could," Nancy said soothingly. "I'm sure they didn't suspect you. They probably talked to everyone the same way."

"Hmmph!" Hannah said indignantly. She rose to her feet and stalked out of the auction house. Nancy trailed after her.

As they crossed the preview rooms, Mr. Rendell stepped out of his office. "Ms. Drew," he called out, "I have that list of names you wanted." Nancy halted briefly to take the list and thanked him. Then she hurried after Hannah.

Outside, Nancy glanced down at the list in her hand. Mr. Rendell had given her not only names but addresses and phone numbers as well. There was only one name Nancy recognized: Risa Palmetto. Risa's was the only name that also appeared on Officer Nomura's list. I've got to check that woman out, Nancy resolved.

"Hannah," Nancy said, heading across the nearly empty parking lot to her Mustang, "I'll meet you at home later. There's a suspect I need to interview."

Hannah looked up and then frowned. "Oh, Nancy," she said in a worried voice. "Look!" She raised her hand and pointed at the Mustang.

"What—" Nancy stopped and examined her car. With a sinking feeling she saw what was troubling Hannah.

The left front tire of Nancy's Mustang was completely flat. Deep gashes sliced across the black rubber, and strips of tread hung off like ribbons.

Someone had slashed Nancy's tire!

7

A Ride into Danger

"Who would do such a thing?" Hannah asked, looking shaken.

"That's an excellent question," Nancy replied. Her eyes scanned the few cars left in the auction house's parking lot. "I'm pretty sure it wasn't a random act. Whoever slashed my tire knew it was my car."

"I wonder if it was someone at the auction," Hannah said.

"It had to be someone who knew I was here," Nancy said. "And I'd guess that if it *was* someone at the auction, it was someone who left early. People don't slash tires while the police are on the scene."

"Maybe it was that man Sather," Hannah said.

"Or Risa Palmetto or Richard Munro or Cyril Bloom or Arianne Stone," Nancy finished with a sigh.

"But why would any of them slash your tire?" Hannah asked.

"Maybe this is another warning," Nancy speculated. "Or maybe someone's trying to slow me down or stop me from the next step in the investigation."

"I don't know, Nancy," Hannah said, "but I'm going back in there to report this to the police."

"Might as well," Nancy agreed. "Meanwhile, I'm going to get to work on this tire. And then I'm going to check out Risa Palmetto."

It took Nancy half an hour to remove the slashed tire, put on her spare, and fill out a police report. Then she headed straight to the address Mr. Rendell had listed for Risa Palmetto.

The address was in a wealthy section called Brookdale, just outside River Heights. Nancy drove for about fifteen minutes before finding it. She pulled up on the circular drive in front of a house that looked as though it had escaped from the set of *Gone with the Wind*—a massive mansion with soaring columns and statues of cherubs scattered among the shrubbery.

Nancy parked behind a large magenta luxury sedan. She half-expected a butler to answer when she rang the bell, but Risa opened the door herself. She was dressed in a lime green satin dressing gown with cascades of ruffles down the front.

"Who are you?" Risa asked bluntly.

"My name is Nancy Drew," Nancy explained. "I met you at Richard Munro's reading the other night. I've been investigating local book thefts, and I wanted to talk to you about your stolen books."

"Oh, don't remind me," Risa said, leading her into the house. "I've been upset about that for weeks!"

Nancy was surprised to see that, despite the grand exterior, the house was somewhat run-down inside. Risa led her to a huge living room furnished with a couch upholstered in a bright orange tiger-stripe print and a worn rug.

"You're thinking it needs some sprucing up, right?" Risa said, guessing Nancy's thoughts. "Well, that's because my darling stepchildren have tied up my husband's entire estate with lawsuits. He left everything to me, and they can't stand it! I tell you, I can barely afford to keep up the house. The truth is"—Risa lowered her voice to a dramatic whisper—"I spend every cent I can on books. And I can't even do that unless the book is a steal."

Odd choice of words, Nancy thought to herself. "That's what I wanted to ask you about, Ms. Palmetto," she said, pulling a small notebook out of her purse. "Which of your books were stolen?"

"*A Boy's King Arthur* and *The Adventures of Robin Hood,* both illustrated by N. C. Wyeth," Risa replied promptly. "First editions—absolutely gorgeous! I'd just had them completely rebound."

"Who rebound them for you?" Nancy asked quickly.

"Why, Leonard Sather, of course," Risa replied. "He's the only bookbinder anyone would use."

Nancy scribbled down Sather's name with interest. "By the way, why did you leave Rendell's auction early today?" she asked.

Risa's eyes narrowed. "I went for one book, and I didn't get it," she said. "There was no point in staying."

"Could I see your collection?" Nancy asked.

Risa beamed at her and led the way to the back of the house, where she flung open a set of French doors. Inside was a large room, the walls covered floor to ceiling with bookshelves.

"I collect children's books," Risa said, "from the eighteenth century to the present day. You can have a look. Just be careful with the old ones."

Nancy browsed the shelves, recognizing many of her favorites from childhood. Risa might be quirky, but she did have a room filled with books Nancy loved. "Do you have a security system here?" Nancy asked.

"Do I look like a fool?" Risa replied. "Of course, I have a security system. I—" She gave a little jump as the phone rang. "I've got to get that," she said. "I'll be right back."

As Risa dashed out, Nancy stood still, studying the room. There were hundreds of books shelved, way too many for her to search for the missing titles. If Risa *had* stolen them, she was far too smart to display them here, anyway, Nancy figured.

Nancy didn't see any cameras or electrical wires around. Probably Risa's system protects the whole house, not just this one room, she thought. She decided to check out the main entrances. Nancy started toward the front of the house, only to be stopped by Risa's voice echoing through the empty halls. "I want that book," Risa was saying. "And I don't care what you have to do to get it!"

Nancy heard Risa slam the receiver down. Seconds later she came striding down the hall, her high heels clicking along the marble floors. "Dealers!" she exclaimed. "They just want my money. So," she continued, abruptly changing the subject, "did you find out how the thief got into my library?"

"It would help if you told me what sort of security system you have," Nancy explained.

"I've got those little plastic whatsits on the doors," Risa answered vaguely.

"Could you show me?" Nancy suggested.

Risa led her around to the back door, which looked out on an unkempt garden. "The alarm is off now," she said, opening the door. She pointed toward the top of the door frame, where Nancy saw a narrow rectangle of white plastic screwed into the wood. On the door, in a matching position, was a similar rectangle of white plastic.

"Oh, you've got a magnetic contact switch," Nancy said, recognizing the commonly used system. "When the magnet on the door comes close to the one on the door frame, the magnetic field closes a switch. When the door opens, the electrical connection is broken, and an alarm goes off. It's supposed to be very reliable."

"Yeah, right," Risa said. "I've got 'em on all the doors and all the windows. But what happens? Two books disappear from my library and not a peep! I called the security people out that day, and they ran tests and said the system works like a charm. Some charm!"

"It probably *was* working," Nancy said thoughtfully. "But obviously someone figured out how to get around it."

Once Risa started talking, it was hard to get her to stop. It was six o'clock by the time Nancy left, but she'd gathered only one more piece of useful information: that Risa didn't use a mark of ownership on her books.

The woman was definitely a suspect, Nancy decided as she got into her car. She appeared to know an awful lot about the other collectors who'd lost books, and her own money troubles gave her a perfect motive for stealing books to add to her collection. And several of the missing books— Cyril's *Peter Pan*, Nancy's *Hound of the Baskervilles*, the *Alice in Wonderland* taken from Rendell's—were titles that would fit Risa's collection perfectly. However, Nancy knew that all the books that were stolen weren't children's books. Would Risa go to the trouble to steal books she didn't collect? Nancy wondered. Maybe she sold

66

them and used the money to buy the titles she wanted.

The interview had also stirred Nancy's curiosity about one more suspect, so she started up her car and headed for Leonard Sather's workshop.

Fortunately, it was only another fifteen minutes up the highway from Brookdale to the little town where Leonard Sather had his workshop. In Oakville Nancy stopped at a gas station pay phone to call home. "Hannah," she said when the housekeeper answered, "I wanted to let you and Dad know I'll be back late. Don't hold dinner for me. I'll pick up something on the way. And if George or Bess call, would you let them know where I am?"

"I'll tell them," Hannah promised. "Thanks for calling."

Rain began to fall as Nancy turned onto Leonard Sather's road. Night was gathering quickly. As she reached the bookbindery, Nancy saw that the farmhouse was dark; only the workshop lights were on. Nancy parked by the barn and, using her flashlight, picked her way across the muddy driveway. She pounded on the workshop door and waited, but no one answered. She pounded harder to be heard above the rain, which began falling more heavily.

The door swung open. "Nancy," Lori Chang cried. "Quick, come in. You're getting soaked."

"I'm here to see Mr. Sather. Is he in?" Nancy explained, slipping gratefully inside.

"He's not back from the auction yet," Lori answered.

But the auction ended hours ago, Nancy thought, and Sather hadn't even stayed for all of it. "Do you expect him back soon?" she asked. "Can I wait?"

Lori frowned. "Well, sure, but you'd better wait upstairs in my place. I'm not supposed to let people in the workshop, remember? I don't want Leonard to have another cow. Come on up and I'll make you a cup of tea. Do you need a pair of dry socks?"

Nancy followed the tall girl up a narrow flight of stairs into a studio apartment that had been built into the rafters of the barn. It was small but cozy, with a kitchenette and a daybed covered with a bright patchwork quilt. Every shelf and every surface was crowded with books, both new and old.

"You want to talk to Leonard about the stolen books?" Lori said as she put a kettle on the stove.

Nancy nodded. "Someone knows I'm investigating this case and has been trying to stop me," she said. Then she told Lori about the threatening message in Richard's book, the theft at the auction house, and her slashed tire.

"Leonard was in both places," Nancy pointed out. "And he left the auction early, before the theft was discovered and the police showed up."

Lori sighed. "I guess you're thinking he might be the thief. If you knew him better, you'd know he couldn't possibly be. Books are so precious to him.''

"Have you had any thefts here in the workshop?" Nancy asked, still suspicious of Sather.

"Well, no," Lori said.

"Hmm. Have you got a list of the books that you've worked on in the last year?" Nancy asked.

"Sure, in the office. I'll get it. Keep an eye on the kettle," Lori said, and she ran back down to the workshop.

When she returned, she gave Nancy a computer printout. "I finally convinced Leonard to get a computer for our office. I'm proud of how organized we are now," she said. "These are all the jobs we've billed for this year."

Nancy scanned the list quickly. She recognized several of the missing titles, including Risa's two books and Cyril Bloom's *Peter Pan*.

When Nancy pointed this out, Lori shrugged. "Leonard's the best bookbinder in the area," she said. "Everybody uses him—that's no coincidence. But all these books were returned to their owners before they were stolen. I can vouch for that."

"I still want to talk to him," Nancy said.

But as the evening passed, Sather did not return. Nancy had a pleasant time chatting with Lori, who fixed a delicious dinner for the two of them. As it grew later, Nancy faced the fact that she wouldn't be interviewing the bookbinder that night.

Finally she said good night to Lori, explaining

that she had a long drive home. Lori led her downstairs and through the workshop to the door.

On the way, Nancy saw a book lying dismantled on a nearby worktable. Next to it was a letter. She recognized the Emerson College crest on the stationery.

Nancy stopped to look more closely. The letter was full of instructions for the book's repair.

And it was signed Arianne Stone.

Why does that girl keep cropping up? Nancy wondered. She showed up at Cyril's for the reading, then she was at Rendell's for the auction. And now here's a letter from her in Leonard Sather's workshop.

Lori opened the workshop door. "At least the rain has stopped," she said. "It's pretty dark out, though. Can you see your way to the car okay?"

"No problem." Nancy fished her pocket flashlight out of her purse. "Thanks again for a nice evening."

After Lori said goodbye and closed the door, Nancy turned on her flashlight, training the beam over the muddy driveway. That's strange, she thought. Those car tracks in the mud—I know they weren't there before. Someone must have pulled into the drive and then driven back out again since I got here.

Maybe it was Sather, she mused. Maybe he came back, saw my car, and left again. Nancy felt a chill go through her as she remembered the warning note and her slashed tire. Was Sather stalking her?

She shone the beam of light around the farmyard but saw nothing else suspicious. The best thing to do, she told herself, would be to get home quickly.

The rain started up again as Nancy drove back toward the highway. She rolled up the windows, concentrating on the road. The pavement was slick beneath her wheels, and she lowered her speed and drove cautiously.

When she stopped for gas, a station attendant warned her that the highway had been blocked by an overturned truck. He gave her directions back to River Heights along smaller country roads.

Nancy turned on the radio to keep herself company as she started down the old river road. She was feeling tired, so she turned the radio up louder. I wish I'd gotten a cup of coffee at that gas station, she thought drowsily. It wasn't very late, but she was having a hard time keeping her eyes open. She felt a little strange and slow.

Then, as Nancy took a curve on the rain-slick road, she felt herself go into a skid. Steer into it, she told herself, but she couldn't seem to react quickly enough. Everything had slowed down as though it were some awful dream.

She could feel the car sliding sideways, but she felt powerless, unable to stop it. Next she heard a massive crashing sound. The car bounced hard and rolled onto its side.

Then everything went black.

8

No Simple Accident

"Can you hear me, miss?" a strange voice asked.

Feeling groggy, Nancy opened her eyes and felt a painful pounding in her head. She shut her eyes again quickly, and bright lights flashed before them.

"Can you hear me?" The voice sounded far away. "Please, we need to know how badly you've been hurt."

Memories of driving back from Sather's workshop came to Nancy. She recalled feeling sleepy and then the Mustang sliding off the road. "I—I'm all right," she said, opening her eyes again. Gingerly, she pushed herself upright.

The voice belonged to a young paramedic in a white uniform, she saw. "Don't move," he said. "We'll help you get out of the car."

Fifteen minutes later Nancy was sitting on a gurney in the back of an ambulance. "I'm fine, really," she told the paramedics. "I have a headache, but I can still drive myself home."

"That's not a good idea," the medic said. "We're going to check you into the hospital for some tests. And I think your car should be looked over by a mechanic before you drive it again."

Nancy felt too exhausted to argue. She lay back on the stretcher. A few seconds after the ambulance began moving, she fell asleep.

"I thought you were supposed to be taking it easy," Carson Drew joked the next morning as he entered Nancy's hospital room. Nancy was fully dressed and pacing the small room like a caged animal.

"Did the doctors say they'd release me?" Nancy asked impatiently.

"On one condition—you must go home and stay in bed for a day," Dr. Dryeberg said, coming into Nancy's room behind her dad. "Our tests showed no concussion or other damage, just a mild case of carbon monoxide poisoning. That's probably what made you so sleepy. But the symptoms of carbon monoxide poisoning take many forms, and they often don't appear for twenty-four hours. If you start to forget things or have trouble talking, I want you back here pronto."

"But, Dad, I need to borrow your car and drive to Emerson to question Arianne Stone," Nancy began. She wanted to find out why the student seemed to show up wherever Nancy's investigation took her.

"No way," Mr. Drew said firmly. "No more car trips for you for the next few days. Especially until we find out why your car was leaking carbon monoxide."

So Nancy spent all Sunday in bed. She felt tired, but still she managed to get some work done on the case. First she called the police and told them about the tire tracks near Sather's barn. Then she got her father to pick up the list of book thefts Officer Nomura had copied for her. Once she had the list of the seven local collectors who'd had books stolen—which included Risa and Cyril— she called George and asked her to keep her eye on Risa and Cyril and check out the five new names. Finally, she called Ned and asked him to question Arianne Stone about why she left the auction early and about the book she'd left at Sather's.

On Monday morning Nancy felt much better. She was glad when the doorbell rang after breakfast and George and Bess walked in. Bess, she noticed, was wearing cutoffs and a white T-shirt, but she still had the pink bow in her hair. And the look on her face was kind of spaced-out and distracted.

"Bess," Nancy said cautiously. "Why are you wearing that pink ribbon in your hair? Isn't it kind of dressy for cutoffs and a T-shirt?"

"A little," Bess admitted, "but Richard loves it. He says it's something only a true romantic would wear. So I've been wearing it every day."

"Feeling better, Nan?" George said, changing the subject.

"I'm fine," Nancy said, and offered her friends orange juice and muffins. Then she brought the two cousins up to date on Saturday's events: the auction, the visits to Risa Palmetto and Leonard Sather, and her late-night car accident. "We still have too many suspects," Nancy concluded. "Leonard Sather, Arianne Stone, Risa Palmetto—"

"Risa sounds more like a victim to me," Bess said. "Broken-hearted, feuding with her husband's family . . ."

"I can't tell," Nancy said. "One minute she's telling me how poor she is, the next she's ordering some dealer to get her a book at any price."

"Oh, yesterday I talked to a few of the collectors who had books stolen," George reported.

"And?" Nancy asked.

"All I can tell is that our thief is pretty smart," George answered. "Some of these collectors had no security systems at all, but others had pretty sophisticated devices."

Nancy looked over at Bess, who was ignoring their conversation and writing furiously in a lined notebook. "I have a feeling another poem is being born," George whispered to Nancy.

Nancy grinned. "What kinds of security systems did they have?" she asked, intent on the case again.

"One collector kept the book that was stolen on

a desk on top of a blotter," George said. "Beneath that blotter is a pressure-mat alarm. The system is designed so that the alarm goes off if you lift an object off the pad."

"Pretty neat," Nancy said. "Did the alarm go off when the book was stolen?"

"Nope," George said. "And the system was working. The police suspect that the thief pressed the book down against the mat and then gradually slid it off while sliding on another object of the same weight, so that the alarm wouldn't sound."

"So the robber knew exactly which book he or she was after, what it weighed, and how to fool the security system," Nancy said. "Clever thief. You know, Risa Palmetto has a magnetic contact system, but she refers to it as 'those little white plastic whatsits.' Either she's a very good actress or she doesn't know anything about security systems."

Nancy reached for a folder on the counter and took out the list Mr. Rendell had given her of collectors interested in *Alice in Wonderland*. She laid it on the table beside Nomura's list of collectors who'd had books stolen. Then she added the printout Lori had given her of all the books Leonard Sather had worked on in the last year. "I'm looking for a connection between these three lists," Nancy explained as she and George studied the names.

"There are twenty-two collectors on Rendell's list, but most are out of state," Nancy continued. "Only Risa appears on both lists, though I'm not sure that means she's the thief."

"But of the seven names on Nomura's list, all of them had books Sather worked on," George pointed out. "There's got to be a connection there."

"You'd think so," Nancy said. "But there aren't many bookbinders around. I'd bet every local collector takes books to Leonard Sather."

Just then Bess looked up, her face radiant. "Sorry, you guys," she said. "But Richard says that when inspiration strikes, you just have to stop everything and give in to the poem. Do you want to hear it?" Before Nancy or George had a chance to refuse, Bess began reading.

"The sky at sunset
Colors galore
You in jeans, me in a gorgeous dress.
I look at the melting chocolate mousse
And remember our love."

This time Bess didn't ask Nancy or George what they thought. Instead she breezed on, "Richard says I've reached a whole new level in my work. In this one, the melting chocolate mousse is a symbol of how Richard and I melt each other's hearts."

George threw Nancy a panicked look, and Nancy knew she had to say something. "Bess," she began, "I think Richard Munro is a good poet and one of the best-looking guys I've ever seen. But you've known him only a week."

"I don't care," Bess said. "It's love."

"Have you even had a date yet?" Nancy asked.

"No," Bess admitted as she nibbled on a blueberry muffin. "Richard's been very busy. But we send each other e-mail at least five times a day. Richard says it's a great literary correspondence."

George sighed. "Bess, every sentence of yours begins with 'Richard says.'"

"But he never actually *says* anything," Nancy added. "He just writes to you."

Bess smiled dreamily. "It's just like a long-distance relationship," Bess said. "And they can be *so* romantic."

"Well, Bloom's isn't all that far away," Nancy pointed out. "So why don't we get there now and see the real, live Richard Munro in the flesh?"

"That's not a bad idea," Bess agreed.

"And maybe Cyril can give us some help on the case," Nancy added.

Bess eagerly led the way into Bloom's. Standing on tiptoe, she gazed around the store. "I don't see Richard," she said, disappointed. "He told me he'd be working today."

"Maybe he'll be in later," Nancy said. "I don't see Cyril either. Let me check his office. If I find him, I'll ask him about Richard."

Nancy walked to the back of the store and found the wooden door to Cyril's office closed. She knocked, but there was no answer.

"No sign of Cyril?" George guessed when Nancy returned.

"None," Nancy said. "But here's Richard."

Richard Munro had just rushed into the bookstore, lugging a large book satchel. Walking swiftly, he headed toward the counter near the cash registers. He'd just reached it when Bess saw him. "Richard!" she called out happily.

Richard turned and gazed coolly at Bess. "Does that look like a man in love?" George whispered to Nancy.

"No," Nancy said in a worried tone. "That doesn't even look like a man in *like.*"

Bess, though, didn't seem bothered. "I can't wait to show you my new poem," she trilled.

"Now's not a good time—" Richard began.

At that moment a lovely young woman with gold-framed glasses came to the counter. "Do either of you work here?" she asked. "I've got a huge reading list for college. Could you help me find some books?"

"Of course," Richard said with his most charming smile. "Bess, I have to help this customer now."

"I understand," Bess said. "I'll wait."

Richard led the young woman to the other side of the store. Bess fidgeted. Then she did something that surprised Nancy. She picked up Richard's satchel and began looking at the books inside.

"Are you spying on the love of your life?" George teased, coming up behind her cousin.

"Of course not," Bess protested. "I just want to find out what Richard's reading so I can spark more conversations with him. It isn't enough just to be soul mates. You need that intellectual . . . *something.*"

"Well, that something doesn't seem to be poetry," Nancy said, looking through the thick volumes Bess had taken from the satchel. "These books aren't poems. These are court reports—collections of legal cases. Dad's got lots of books like these in his office."

"And look at all these little yellow stickers he's put on the pages," George added.

"Maybe he's applying to law school," Bess said. "Richard's very bright."

Nancy pulled out her pocket notebook and began copying down the titles of the books, their volume numbers, and the page numbers where the yellow stickers were. "Why are you doing that?" Bess asked.

"Just a hunch," Nancy replied, slipping the pad back in her purse. "It's too interesting to ignore."

"Bess," George said softly, "I think we'd better put these books back." Richard was striding toward them, and he looked furious. Bess frantically shoved books back into the bag, but she wasn't fast enough.

"What do you think you're doing?" Richard demanded. "How dare you snoop through my things?"

"I—I just wanted to see what you were reading," Bess stammered, "so we'd have more things to talk about."

"Fine," Richard said coldly. "Let's talk about how you're invading my privacy."

80

Bess paused for a moment, lips trembling. Then she covered her face with her hands and fled from the store. George glared at Richard and then ran out after Bess. Nancy followed right on her heels.

They found Bess standing by George's car, tears welling up in her eyes. "He hates me," she wailed.

"He doesn't hate you," Nancy said, putting her arm around Bess's shoulders. "He's just a very private person."

"It's no big loss, anyway," George said, opening the car. "He doesn't seem like a very nice guy."

Bess flung herself onto the backseat, sniffing and wiping her eyes. "You don't understand!" she insisted. "I think we were made for each other."

"Bess," Nancy said tactfully, "if Richard is really Mr. Right, he won't stay mad over such a little thing. You'll make up."

That seemed to comfort Bess, and they got back to the Marvins' house without another outburst. Nancy glanced at her watch as George pulled up the drive. "Can I use your phone, Bess?" she asked. "I promised Ned I'd check in and see what he's found on Arianne."

"Sure," Bess snuffled.

Nancy quickly made her call to Ned. "I've got big news," he told her. "They discovered another book theft at the library. They *think* the book disappeared Sunday morning—on Arianne's shift. There's no evidence, so she can't be charged, but this morning Ms. Buller asked her to resign. Even if she didn't steal the book, she wasn't doing her job properly. She should have been able to prevent the theft."

"Where is she now?" Nancy asked.

"No one knows," Ned answered. "Ms. Buller fired her at nine. When David went to talk to her at noon, her room in the dorm was completely cleaned out."

At about three-thirty, George and Nancy checked in at the garage where the blue Mustang had been towed. They found the Mustang high up on the pneumatic lift. Beneath it, the mechanic, Jane Morris, was squinting up at its undercarriage.

"How's the patient?" Nancy asked.

Jane grinned at her. "Not great, but she'll survive. I've ordered a new bumper for you and fixed a hole in the radiator. How are *you* doing?"

"Fine," Nancy said. "But the doctors think a carbon monoxide leak made me fall asleep at the wheel. Did you spot a leak?"

"No," Jane said. "Let me check again." Using a handheld light, she examined the underside of the car. "Hmmm—a hole in the exhaust pipe," she said. Then she lowered the light and, with a concerned expression, looked Nancy in the eye. "This hole wasn't caused by normal wear and tear. It's perfectly round."

"What do you mean?" Nancy asked.

"I mean someone cut this hole," Jane said gravely. "It was no accident that you passed out from carbon monoxide poisoning. Someone was trying to kill you!"

9

A Clue at Last

"Someone cut a hole in my exhaust pipe?" Nancy asked the mechanic.

"Are you sure?" George asked.

"See for yourself," Jane Morris replied. She shone her light over a perfectly round hole about the size of a quarter. "You can't get a hole like that unless you deliberately cut one," she told Nancy.

"I wonder when the hole was cut," Nancy said.

"How long would it take for the carbon monoxide to take effect and make a person pass out?" George asked the mechanic.

"I'd guess twenty minutes to half an hour," Jane replied. "Until you get drowsy, you don't notice anything. Carbon monoxide has no scent, color, or taste. It's a silent, invisible killer."

"I felt fine when I drove to the auction house," Nancy remembered. "And I wasn't sleepy when I went to Risa's or out to Leonard Sather's. It was only on the way home from the farm that I started to feel it."

"How long were you at the farm?" George asked.

"Over an hour," Nancy answered.

"That would be plenty of time for someone who knew what they were doing to cut this hole," Jane said.

Then Nancy remembered the tire marks beside her car. "And I have good idea of who that someone is," she said grimly.

After thanking Jane Morris, Nancy told her she'd pick up the car later in the week.

"So, are you going to tell me or not?" George prodded Nancy as they drove back to the Drews' house. "Who did that to your car?"

"Well, there weren't that many cars on the road when I drove to the workshop," Nancy said.

"And," George said, waiting for Nancy to go on.

"And he was late coming home that night," Nancy continued, thinking out loud.

"Who?" George asked impatiently.

"And he certainly has the motive. Money is always a big motivator for any crime."

"Nancy!" George exclaimed, making her friend jump in the seat beside her.

"What?"

"Are you going to tell me who your suspect is or not?" George asked in an exasperated tone.

"Oh, sure," Nancy replied calmly. "Leonard Sather, of course."

"Finally," George said. "The suspense was killing me."

That evening at dinner, Nancy's dad looked at her with concern. "Are you sure you're feeling all right?" he asked. "I hope the mechanic fixed that leak."

"The car will be fine and I'm fine—really, Dad," Nancy said, smiling. But she didn't tell her father about the mechanic's discovery. If he knew someone had tried to hurt her, he might order her off the case, and she felt she was getting too close to give up now.

"So tell me about this mystery of yours," Mr. Drew said as he started his dinner.

"I'd love to. In fact, I need your help." Nancy sketched in the details of the case thus far, including her suspicions about Leonard Sather, then told her dad about the law books Richard Munro had been carrying. "It seems like such an odd thing for a poet to be lugging around," she said. "I wrote down the titles and some of the case numbers that Richard had marked. Could you find out what's in those books?"

Mr. Drew nodded. "Leave your notes on my desk," he said. "I'll see what I can find in the firm's library."

The phone rang then, and Nancy offered to get it. She nearly dropped the receiver in surprise when she heard the voice on the other end.

It was Leonard Sather.

"I have to talk to you," he said gruffly.

"Why now?" Nancy said, immediately suspicious. "You've avoided talking to me all week."

"Well, I changed my mind," he said. "I want to talk. Can you come out here?"

Nancy felt her hand shaking. What if Leonard Sather was the one who put that deadly hole in her exhaust pipe? "Can't you tell me over the phone?" she suggested.

There was silence on the other end. When the bookbinder spoke again, his voice had grown quieter.

"Listen, I've lost two rare, irreplaceable books out of my own workshop," he said. "Right from under my own nose. No one knows, not even Lori. If word gets out that books aren't safe here, I'll lose half my business.

"That's why I was angry that first time I saw you," he added. "I'd heard that there'd been thefts in the area, and I thought you could have been the thief. Or you could have started some kind of rumor about my shop."

"So what made you change your mind?" Nancy asked guardedly.

"The police have been around, checking out those tire tracks you saw in my driveway," the bookbinder explained. "They told me who you are. They also told me about your accident. It doesn't sound like an accident to me."

His voice sounded concerned, not threatening, but still Nancy didn't trust him. "Someone punctured my exhaust pipe," she admitted. Then, going on the offensive, she asked, "Was it you? Were those tire tracks yours?"

She was surprised to hear Leonard Sather chuckle. "You've got the wrong man," he replied. "I don't drive. I never have. You can check that out. I took a bus back from River Heights Saturday evening, and it got caught in traffic—there was a wreck out on the highway. I got home about an hour after Lori says you left."

"Well, *someone* drove into your driveway while I was there," Nancy insisted. "I saw the car tracks. If it wasn't you, who could it have been?"

"Who knew you were coming to my place?" the bookbinder asked her.

"Only my family and my two best friends," she replied.

"Maybe somebody followed you here," he suggested.

"Maybe," Nancy said, considering. It would have been difficult to see a car in the rain. She'd been at Risa's house and at the auction before that. Could someone have followed her all the way to Oakville?

"This is getting serious," Leonard Sather went on. "Someone clearly wants to stop you from asking questions. I think I can help you find some answers. Could you come out here?"

"All right, I'll come in the morning," Nancy said. "But I'd like to bring my friends George and Bess along with me. Will Lori be there?"

"Yes," the bookbinder said with a sigh. "We won't be alone—you'll be safe. Can you come at ten?"

"Ten o'clock," Nancy agreed. But as she hung up the phone, she found herself hoping that she and her friends weren't walking into a trap.

The next morning was beautiful, and the ride in George's car out to Oakville on winding back roads was far more pleasant than Nancy's last country ride had been. On the way Nancy pointed out to Bess and George the spot where her car had crashed.

Bess shuddered. "Do you still think Sather is the one who tampered with your car?" she said.

"I don't know," Nancy answered. "As he said, anyone could have followed me from the auction."

"By the way, how's *your* investigation going, Love Detective?" George asked Bess. "Any news on who Cyril Bloom's Dark Lady was?"

"I've got some very interesting leads," Bess replied with a coy smile. "I've given up on the Risa angle. But I did do some snooping in Cyril's office, and you wouldn't believe what I saw." Before George or Nancy could respond, Bess said, "There was this picture of him when he was younger with this totally beautiful dark-haired woman. Cyril was pretty gorgeous back then himself. The woman has *got* to be the Dark Lady in his poetry, the one he was madly in love with. I'm sure of it. Now I just have to find out who she was."

"Well, let me know," Nancy said as George

turned the car into Leonard Sather's drive. "As they say, love is one of the greatest mysteries of all. Sounds like you're getting close to cracking it, Bess."

Lori was waiting to greet them. "Oh, Nancy, I'm so glad you're all right," she said. "I couldn't believe it when I heard that you'd crashed on Saturday night."

Lori took the girls into the workshop. Leonard Sather was bent over a worktable, carefully trimming away the old binding on a fire-damaged book. He looked up, and for the first time Nancy saw him smile. It was an apologetic smile, but it utterly transformed his craggy face.

Lori made them all a pot of tea, and they sat down to discuss the case. Nancy asked the bookbinder to give her every bit of information he could about the books stolen from his workshop as well as the books that had been stolen from his clients.

"I've been racking my brain trying to come up with a common link," Mr. Sather said, "and I can't. Each stolen book came to me from a different client. They were all different types of books. There was no link between them, and I'm a book man, so I'd have noticed a link."

"Could they have all come from one collection at some point in the past?" Lori asked him.

He shrugged. "That's possible," he said. "But it would have been a very wide-ranging collection, not a scholarly one. I'd say it was built by someone who loves to read, has lots of different interests, and is collecting for pleasure, not financial investment."

"Could the books have had some identifying mark of ownership?" Nancy asked, remembering her conversation with William Laws at the auction.

Leonard Sather looked impressed. "You've done your homework, Ms. Drew," he said. "And you're right. I can't remember any marks offhand, but if there were any irregularities, I would have noted them. Let me get my files."

The bookbinder went to his office and brought back several handsomely bound old-fashioned ledgers. He opened the first one and showed it to Nancy. Inside were rows of neatly penciled notes for each book he had repaired.

"I always make extensive notes about the physical condition of the books," he explained. "I'm an obsessive old fussbudget, I guess. But it protects me if a customer tries to claim a book was in better condition when it arrived here than it really was. This way no one can claim that I damaged a book."

"So if there were any unusual marks in the books," Lori put in, "Leonard would have recorded it."

"What if we each take a ledger and find the notes for each of the stolen books?" Nancy suggested. "Then we can compare them to see if they have anything in common."

Going through all the thick ledgers took Mr. Sather, Lori, Nancy, Bess, and George over an hour. First they located the stolen books in the ledgers, then they pored over the bookbinder's careful notes.

"I don't see ownership marks recorded for any of these," Lori said with a sigh. "No bookplates, no initials, no stamps."

"But a mark of ownership could be something more subtle," Nancy said. "Like the small ink stain Leonard noted on the back page of a copy of *Wuthering Heights*. Do any of the books you're looking up have a small ink stain there?"

Lori shook her head. So did Bess, George, and Mr. Sather.

"This copy of *Huckleberry Finn* had wax on the corner of the binding and a cross inked in at the top of the title page," Mr. Sather reported. "Both of those things could be deliberate marks."

But none of the other books had them.

"What about a pinhole on page four, line four?" Bess said dubiously. "That's what you marked down for Risa's *King Arthur* book, Mr. Sather. Could a mark of ownership be something so small and hidden?"

"Could be," Mr. Sather said cautiously.

"I've got a pinhole on page four, line four, of this book, too," George said excitedly.

"So do I," Nancy said. "This could be it! Let's look at the others."

They scoured the notes. Six other books were also marked as having pinholes, but for several of the stolen volumes, no holes were noted.

"With something so small," Mr. Sather said, "I could have missed it on the other titles, especially since I wasn't specifically looking for it. I'd say that's your mark of ownership, all right. It's exactly the sort of thing a collector would do. It's discreet enough that it won't harm the book, but it clearly identifies it as part of a particular collection." He looked at Nancy. "Good detective work, wouldn't you say, Ms. Drew?"

"Yes, I would," replied Nancy. "Three cheers for Bess for finding the pinhole. That was like finding a needle in a haystack."

Bess grinned from ear to ear as everyone cheered, including Mr. Sather. Nancy could have hugged the old grouch. Finally this case was going somewhere!

"So it's quite likely that all these stolen books could have come from one collection," Nancy said. "Now we just have to figure out whose collection it was."

Mr. Sather rubbed his chin. "I can ask the people I know in the business if they've ever heard of that mark of ownership," he suggested. "Cyril might know or William Laws. I'll make a few calls."

But just as he moved to the phone, the sound of an old engine could be heard grinding up the driveway. "Now who's that?" Mr. Sather said, scowling. He crossed over to the window.

"It's just Arianne," Lori said. "She phoned earlier to say she was coming to pick up her book."

"Arianne Stone?" Nancy said, sitting up quickly. "You know, I can't help thinking this is a long way for an Emerson College library book."

"This is a private job," Lori answered. "The book belongs to Arianne, not to the library. It's that book there by your elbow."

Outside, Nancy could hear Arianne gun the motorcycle engine twice, then turn it off.

As Lori went to the door, Nancy reached over to pick up the book Arianne had come for. She saw that it was an old edition of A. A. Milne's *Winnie the Pooh*.

On a hunch, Nancy opened the book to page four. There was a pinhole—precisely on line four.

Nancy stared at the tiny hole, her mind racing. This book belonged to the same collection as the other books that had been stolen.

Was this one of the stolen books? And if so, why did Arianne now think it was hers?

10

A Voice from the Dead?

Arianne Stone came into the workshop, carrying her motorcycle helmet under her arm. She smiled at Lori. Then her smile froze when she saw Nancy sitting behind Lori.

Arianne's eyes lit on the book in Nancy's hands, and color rushed into her face.

"I've come for my book," Arianne announced, her voice sounding tough.

"Is it *your* book?" Nancy asked. She did not put the volume down.

The red-haired girl put her hand on her hip. "So you think I stole this one too, Drew?" she said. "You're as bad as the people at the library. You have no evidence. You just don't like me."

"This is my evidence," Nancy replied, standing up and pointing to the open page. "The pinhole. Page four, line four."

Arianne turned to Leonard Sather. "What is she talking about?" she asked angrily.

94

"Several of the books stolen recently have that mark of ownership, Arianne," Mr. Sather said. "We believe it means that they were all in the same collection at one point."

"Yes, and whose collection was it?" Nancy asked Arianne.

The girl moved forward suddenly and snatched *Winnie the Pooh* out of Nancy's hands. "I don't know about any pinhole," she declared. "I do know whose collection this came out of, though: my aunt Lily's. She gave this book to me."

"Can you prove it?" Nancy demanded.

"As a matter of fact I can." Arianne opened the book's front cover. She showed Nancy a beautifully penned inscription on the inside cover: "To my darling Piglet with love from Aunt Lily."

"I'm Piglet," Arianne stated gruffly.

In another circumstance Nancy would have laughed out loud to hear such an absurd statement from this offbeat girl. Right now, however, it was no laughing matter. The sight of the inscription troubled Nancy for some reason.

"Anyone could have that nickname," Nancy pointed out, crossing her arms.

Arianne put down the book and took her wallet from a zippered pocket in her leather jacket. She searched through the billfold, then slipped out a well-worn photograph. She handed it to Nancy.

The photo showed a beautiful dark-haired woman holding a very young child on her lap. The woman looked like an older, elegant version of

95

Arianne. The pink-cheeked child, with her thatch of red hair, was clearly Arianne herself.

Nancy turned the photograph over. It was inscribed "To Arianne from Aunt Lily" in the same old-fashioned-looking script.

Nancy handed the picture back to Arianne. "I'll be honest with you," Nancy said. "There have been quite a few book thefts in this area besides those at Emerson. I have several suspects at this point, and you're one of them. You turn up everywhere a book has gone missing. You were at Rendell's auction—"

"So? I love books," Arianne said, interrupting. "I always go to Rendell's book auctions just to look."

"But how did you get invited to Richard Munro's poetry reading?" Nancy asked.

Arianne glared at Nancy. "I happened to meet Mr. Bloom one day when I was browsing in his store," she said sharply. "He gave me an invitation. He was handing them out pretty freely. Even *you* got one."

Nancy sensed that Arianne was not only angry, but also hurt that she was being accused of stealing. "Arianne," she said more gently, "if you are innocent, I'd like to prove it. But you've got to help me."

Arianne took a deep breath. Nancy saw that she was near to tears.

"I was a suspect myself until today," Mr. Sather suddenly spoke up. "Join the club, Piglet." He smiled, obviously trying to put the girl at ease.

"What do you want from me?" Arianne said to Nancy in a somewhat sullen voice.

"Well, for starters, why don't you sit down?" said Mr. Sather with gruff kindness. Arianne sunk silently into a chair.

"I'll make another pot of tea," Lori said brightly. She slipped off up the stairs.

Nancy sat near Arianne and said to her, "Your *Winnie the Pooh* seems to be connected to the other books that were stolen. We believe they all have the same mark of ownership—this pinhole on page four, line four. That may mean they were all in the same collection once. Is your aunt Lily a collector?"

"She was. She's dead now," Arianne said quietly.

Nancy paused. "I'm sorry," she said. Then, clearing her throat, she went on. "Here's a list of all the stolen books we know about so far. Is it possible these were all in your aunt's collection?" She handed the list to Arianne.

The girl looked over the list and bit her lip. "I can't say for sure," she said slowly. "I never saw Aunt Lily's collection when it was all together. But these seem like books she could have had. Children's books, history books, nineteenth-century literature—those are all things my aunt loved."

Arianne handed the list back to Nancy. "I can tell you one thing for certain," she went on. "All the books stolen from the Emerson library's rare book room used to belong to the Lily Truscott collection."

"You've known that all along?" Nancy said in surprise. "Did you tell Ms. Buller?"

Arianne shook her head. "I never told anyone," she admitted. "They already thought I'd stolen the books. If I told them that information, it would only have made them more certain than ever."

"How did you know the books came from your aunt's collection?" George spoke up.

"My mother gave Aunt Lily's books to Emerson College after my aunt died," Arianne explained. "She shouldn't have—she should have saved them for me. Aunt Lily would've wanted her to." Nancy saw the anger flash in Arianne's eyes again.

"When I started school at Emerson, I decided to find out where the books were," the red-haired girl continued. "I did some detective work of my own." Arianne glanced up at Nancy with an attempt at a smile. "Some of the books are still at Emerson," she continued. "But many others were sold years ago. I've been told that's standard procedure when a library inherits books—they take what they want and sell the rest. But it really bugs me that the collection wasn't kept together."

Did it bug Arianne enough for her to steal the missing books? Nancy wondered. Aloud, she only said, "Do you know who bought the books?"

Arianne shook her head. "They were sold in bits and pieces over the years," she said, "to various book dealers, charity sales, other libraries . . ."

Nancy remembered the shelf full of nineteenth-century books missing from River Heights Community College. The pieces of this puzzle were certainly fitting together now.

"It seems to me," Nancy said, watching for Arianne's reaction, "that someone wants to put your aunt Lily's collection back together. And that person's willing to commit several crimes to do it."

"And willing to threaten Nancy's life," George added. Arianne looked up at her in horror.

"Now, Arianne," Nancy said, "think hard. Do you know anyone who would have a motive for putting the collection together again?"

"Besides me, you mean?" the red-haired girl said with a shrewd smile. Then she sighed. "Look, I don't know. I was just a kid when Aunt Lily died. I never really got to know her. I think the person you need to ask is my mom."

"Can you arrange for me to speak to her?" Nancy asked.

"I'll try," Arianne said. "I should warn you, though, that my mom and Aunt Lily didn't get along. Mom never talks about Aunt Lily to me, except to say that I'm too much like her. Wild, she means. But maybe I can persuade her to talk to you about Lily. Should I go call her?"

Nancy nodded. Mr. Sather said, "The phone is in the office." He pointed to a small side room off the workshop.

While Arianne was on the phone, Lori came back downstairs with the tea and handed cups around. Nancy took a cup and inhaled the tea's peppermint scent. She realized that her whole body was tense, and she told herself to relax. The case had really broken open this afternoon. But there were still so many things to find out.

A few minutes later Arianne came back into the room. "My mother said she'd talk to you," she told Nancy. "I told her about the thefts. Is seven o'clock tonight all right? Mom's going to be out until then."

George looked at Nancy and said apologetically, "My family and Bess's are having a cookout tonight. We won't be able to drive you, Nan. And your dad doesn't want you to drive yourself yet."

"That's okay," Arianne said, "I'll drive you to my mom's house, Nancy."

"On your bike?" Nancy asked her.

Arianne laughed. "I'll borrow my friend's car. Can I pick you up at six-thirty?"

Nancy nodded and said, "I'll write down my address."

Nancy reached for her notebook on the work-table behind her. As she did so, her eyes fell on Arianne's copy of *Winnie the Pooh*. The cover was still lying open to Lily Truscott's inscription.

There's something familiar about that handwriting, Nancy thought. It's been bugging me ever since Arianne showed it to me.

She narrowed her eyes, forcing herself to concentrate. And then it came to her.

The old-fashioned, elegant script was in the exact same handwriting as the mysterious message written in Richard's book!

Nancy stared in shock at the inscription. Lily

Truscott's handwriting was identical, there was no doubt about it. But Lily Truscott had been dead for years!

There had to be a rational explanation, Nancy told herself. And yet the only one she could think of made no sense at all.

Had she received a threat from a dead woman?

11

A Blueprint for Crime

"Do you have a photocopier here?" Nancy asked Leonard Sather as she eyed the inscription in Arianne Stone's book. "I'd like to make a copy of this, if I can."

"There's a small copier in my office," Mr. Sather replied. Nancy took the *Winnie the Pooh* and stepped into the bookbinder's office.

As she put the rare book down upon the copier's glass top, she allowed herself a shiver of fear. How could she explain a threat from a woman who'd been dead for years?

George and Bess were getting ready to go when Nancy returned. The three girls said goodbye to Lori, Arianne, and Mr. Sather, then went out to their car. Once they pulled out of the driveway, Nancy tersely told her friends about the two matching inscriptions.

"That's so spooky," Bess said. "It's like Lily

Truscott is coming back from the dead to make sure her collection gets back together."

"You know I don't believe in ghosts, Bess," Nancy said firmly.

"There's got to be a rational explanation for this," George said as she stopped at a crossroad. "But who would want to copy a dead woman's handwriting?"

Nancy gazed out the window into the thick forest of trees. "Something strange is going on here, and we're still a long way from figuring it all out."

At exactly six-thirty, Arianne Stone pulled up in front of the Drews' house, driving a red pickup truck. Nancy ran out and hopped in beside her. "Next stop, Mom's house," Arianne said as she stepped on the gas. "Actually, Aunt Lily's old house, too."

"They grew up there?" Nancy asked.

"My grandfather owned it," Arianne explained. "His will left the house to both sisters, but while my mom went off to college, at Emerson, Lily stayed in the house. When Mom finished college, she refused to move in because of Lily's lifestyle."

"Her lifestyle?" Nancy asked curiously.

Arianne grinned. "To me it sounds like it was a lot of fun," she said. "But my mother sees things differently. Most of Lily's friends were actors, musicians, writers, and artists. They were always flying in from Europe or Asia and staying for a month or two. Lily was known for throwing great parties. And according to Mom, none of Lily's friends held respectable jobs, but they all brought Lily books."

Arianne's smile faded as she continued. "Then Lily had the bad luck to be on the same road as a drunk driver. No one survived the crash. She was young—only thirty years old."

"It must have been hard on your mom," Nancy said.

"I think it hurt her worse than she ever lets on," Arianne said. "When Lily died, Mom moved into the house and got rid of all of Lily's possessions. She says she did that because she was so angry at Lily. But I think it was because she couldn't bear to see so many reminders of her."

Arianne pulled up in front of a big two-story wooden house with a wraparound porch. "This must have been quite a place for a party," Nancy said, getting out of the truck.

"That's what I think," Arianne agreed. "Don't suggest that to my mother, though. She likes a neat, orderly, quiet life." Arianne grinned at Nancy. "She can't quite figure out how she wound up with me for a daughter. But sometimes, the way she looks at me, I know I remind her of Lily."

Nancy followed Arianne up the wide wooden stairs to the front door. Arianne opened the door and led the way into a long wood-paneled front hall. She stood at the bottom of the curving stairway and called up, "Mom, we're here."

Then Arianne led Nancy into a large, airy living room, decorated with tall potted plants and a few pieces of simple, elegant furniture. "Have a seat," she told Nancy. "I'll go get some iced tea."

Nancy sat down, and a few seconds later Mrs. Stone entered the room. She looked a lot like Arianne, only with honey-colored hair pulled back into a smooth knot. "You're Nancy Drew," Mrs. Stone said, reaching out to shake Nancy's hand. "And you have some questions about my sister, Lily?"

"That's right," Nancy said. "I'm particularly curious about the last years of her life—who her friends were, what she was doing, and anything you might remember about her book collection."

Mrs. Stone seated herself on the couch. "I'm afraid there isn't much I can tell you about that time," Mrs. Stone began as Arianne brought in a tray with iced tea and tall glasses. "Lily and I weren't speaking then. In fact, I did my best to ignore her friends and everything else about her. We had our differences, you see."

"Did Lily leave any letters?" Nancy asked.

Mrs. Stone sipped her tea. "After Lily died I gave her books to Emerson's library," she said quietly. "Her letters . . . I burned those." She looked down, as though regretting her actions.

"Do you remember any of the titles of her books?" Nancy asked.

"Not a one," Mrs. Stone said with a soft laugh. "Lily had hundreds of books, you see. But I believe I made a list. The donation to Emerson was a charitable tax deduction. I had to list all of the books for that year's tax forms."

Nancy felt her heart speed up with excitement. "Do you still have that list?" she asked.

"You must have those old tax records somewhere," Arianne urged her mother. "You know that every scrap of paper that's ever entered this house has been labeled, filed, and cross-indexed." Arianne looked over at Nancy. "I sometimes think that's how I wound up wanting to be a librarian—I inherited Aunt Lily's love of books *and* my mother's love of organizing."

Mrs. Stone sighed. "Those files are somewhere up in the attic," she said. "But it may take me a while to unearth them."

"If you don't mind looking for them, I'll wait," Nancy said.

Twenty minutes later Mrs. Stone returned with a sheaf of typewritten pages. "You can borrow these," she said as she handed them to Nancy.

"Thank you," Nancy said. "I'll make copies and send the originals back to you." She glanced quickly at the list. As Mrs. Stone had said, Lily must have had hundreds of books—the list was several pages long. It would take a while to read through it.

"There's just one thing," Mrs. Stone said hesitantly. Nancy looked up at her. "If you do learn anything about my sister or her books, would you let me know? I—I wish now that I *did* have more to remember Lily by."

"I will," Nancy promised. "And that's all the more reason to solve this mystery."

It was nearly nine o'clock when Arianne dropped Nancy off at her house. Nancy immediately called Bess and George to tell them what she'd found. Bess's line was busy, but George picked up on the first ring.

"Any luck with Mrs. Stone?" George asked.

"I've got a list of all the books in Lily Truscott's collection!" Nancy said triumphantly.

"Are our stolen books on it?" George asked.

"I haven't had a chance to read it all yet," Nancy said. "But could you tell Bess the news if you talk to her? I called her, but her line's busy."

"Still?" George groaned. "I was talking to her a half-hour ago, and suddenly she had to hang up to go on-line with Richard. Another poem had struck."

"So the romance is going strong?" Nancy asked.

"They're actually having a date tomorrow," George reported.

"As in, 'get together in person'?" Nancy joked.

"Yup," George said. "They're meeting for breakfast. Not exactly the most romantic time of day, but Bess is acting as though Richard asked her to the prom." She paused. "Nan, I'm worried about Bess."

"I'm still not sure about Richard Munro myself," Nancy confessed. "I suspect that the only thing that matters to him is Richard Munro. But if he's good to Bess, I'll overlook it. Anyway, I'd better go. I want to look at this book list."

The two friends said good night and promised to check in with each other the next day. Then Nancy went to her room and curled up on her bed.

She flipped through her notebook to the page where she'd written the titles of the stolen books. Then she spread out Mrs. Stone's list. She began hunting through the long list for each stolen title.

Forty minutes later Nancy sat up and happily hugged her knees to her chest. Mrs. Stone's list confirmed her hunch: Every book that had been stolen had once belonged to Lily Truscott. Every book, that is, except her own *Hound of the Baskervilles*.

Nancy spent the next morning at the police station, comparing notes with Lieutenant Walker. First she told him about the mark of ownership. Then she showed him the list Mrs. Stone had given her and her own list of stolen books.

Lieutenant Walker read through Nancy's list. He stopped as he came to the *Alice in Wonderland* that had been stolen from Rendell's.

"So this book *is* linked to the other book thefts," he said. "And just when we thought we'd solved that one. There's a young employee at Rendell's who's currently our main suspect."

"Did you find his fingerprints?" Nancy asked.

"The fingerprints we found in the preview room didn't match his," Lieutenant Walker answered. "But this guy had access to Rendell's computer system, and he knew the password for the alarm on the preview room. But he couldn't have stolen all these other books—he just returned from a six-month trip abroad. Several of these books were stolen while he was out of the country."

"Did anyone else have access to Rendell's computer system?" Nancy asked. "Any outsider?"

Lieutenant Walker looked surprised. "Why, yes, as a matter of fact," he said. "Just after the security system was put in, Mr. Rendell had trouble getting his password to work, he told me. So he says he had a friend look at it." Walker stopped to check his notes. "A Cyril Bloom. This Bloom guy apparently has a similar system at his bookstore. Bloom came over with his assistant, Richard Munro, and showed Rendell how the passwords work."

Nancy sat up. "So Bloom and Munro knew the password?" she asked breathlessly.

"No," the lieutenant said, "Mr. Rendell says Bloom told him to change the password after he left, so the system would remain secure. Rendell assures me that he changed it then and has changed it periodically ever since. He insists there's no way anyone except his own staff could know the current password."

Nancy sighed. "So we're back to square one again," she said, feeling discouraged.

Nancy returned home from the police station at one o'clock, after spending two hours reviewing transcripts of the police interviews on the day of the auction theft. The officers had interviewed about sixty people, including Rendell's employees. But none of the interviews brought her any closer to solving the riddle of the rare books.

After making herself a sandwich, Nancy decided to check in with her friends. She called Bess first. Mrs. Marvin said that Bess still hadn't come home from her breakfast with Richard. Well, maybe Bess's romance is picking up, Nancy thought as she hung up.

Next Nancy tried George and got a busy signal. She was about to dial the number a second time when her father walked in. "What are you doing home from work so early?" Nancy asked, surprised.

"I wanted to talk to you," her father said. "I've got something you should see."

Carson Drew took a pile of photocopied papers from his briefcase. "I copied the pages that Richard Munro marked in those law books," he said. "It's fascinating what today's young poets are reading."

"What?" Nancy asked, intrigued.

Her father handed her the pages. "These are records from appeals courts," he said. "In each one, a judge reviews a trial verdict and the facts of the case. The trials Munro marked took place at various times over the last ten years, all in different parts of the country."

"So what do they have in common?" Nancy asked.

Leaning on the kitchen counter, Mr. Drew

began to tick off details on his fingers. "Each case involved a theft," he said. "And each case involved a thief who made a plea bargain, confessing in exchange for a lighter sentence. In all of these cases, the judge summarizes the thief's confession. The summary basically explains how these thieves committed their robberies."

Nancy stared at her father. "That means that someone could learn how to get away with stealing by reading these cases."

"Right," he said. "Every one of these pages is a virtual blueprint for how to crack a security system. Listen to this, for example." Mr. Drew picked up a page and began to read:

"Jones had visited the house before as a delivery man and learned that the house was protected by a magnetic switch system. He waited until no one was home, then returned to the house with a compass, and ran it around the door frame. That told him where the poles of the magnetic switch were. Once he located the switch, he held a larger magnet to that point while his partner jimmied the lock and opened the door. As long as Jones held the magnet in place, the alarm system never knew that the door was opened."

Nancy looked at her father, her eyes wide with excitement. "That's how our thief got into Risa Palmetto's house!" she said. "She has a system just like that."

She leaned over to skim other cases. "This is amazing," she said. "Here are dozens of ways to break computerized password systems. There's also a case here that tells how to get around a pressure mat, exactly the way our book thief did. There are even ways to fool infrared systems, like Rendell's has."

Carson Drew cleared his throat. "As I said, it's very interesting reading for a young poet."

Nancy frowned. "So Richard Munro isn't just a young poet," she said. "I bet he's the book thief. Which means he's the one who tampered with my car."

Then Nancy remembered something that made the blood drain from her face. "Oh, Dad," she said urgently. "Bess is with him *right now!*"

12

A Friend in Danger

"I've got to call Bess again," Nancy told her father urgently. She dialed Bess's number but got only the Marvins' answering machine, meaning that no one was home.

Nancy left a message, asking Bess to call her back as soon as possible, then dialed George. George wasn't home either. While Nancy was talking to the Faynes' machine, the Drews' doorbell rang. Mr. Drew went to answer it.

A few seconds later, George rushed into the kitchen, looking every bit as worried as Nancy felt. "Something's happened to Bess," George said breathlessly. "She was supposed to meet me an hour ago to shop for a birthday present for my mom. She never showed."

Nancy felt her own fear sharpen. "It's not like Bess to blow off a shopping trip," she said.

"No, it isn't," George agreed in a grim tone.

"I called Bess at about one, after I got back from

113

the police station," Nancy said. "Her mother said she was still out with Richard. That's an awfully long breakfast."

Standing behind George, Mr. Drew shot Nancy a grave look. Nancy nodded and turned to George. "I'd better tell you what else I found out," she said reluctantly. She went on to explain what she and her father had just learned.

"Richard was awfully mean when he saw Bess looking at those law books," Nancy concluded. "I'm sure he's behind the book thefts."

George dropped miserably into a chair. "If Richard's the book thief, then he's also the one who punctured your exhaust pipe," she said. "If he thinks Bess is onto him, he could have tampered with her car—"

"Or hurt her and left her somewhere," Nancy finished.

"If only we knew where they went this morning," George said, clenching her fists. "It would at least give us a place to start looking."

"Wait a minute," Nancy said. "Did they arrange this date through e-mail?"

"I think so, but I'm not a hundred percent sure," George replied.

"Well, if they did set up the date on-line, there may be a record of it on Bess's computer," Nancy explained. "Do you and Bess still have keys to each other's houses?"

"I've got hers on my key ring," George replied.

"Then let's see what we can find," Nancy said, hopping up eagerly from her chair.

Mr. Drew was leaning against the kitchen doorway. "Hang on a minute," he said. "Let's not jump to conclusions. Too many things aren't accounted for here."

"Like what, Dad?" Nancy asked.

"If Richard Munro is behind all the thefts, how would he have traced *your* whereabouts so closely, Nan?" her dad pointed out. "How would he have known you were going out to Sather's bookbindery on Saturday night, for example?"

Nancy took a deep breath. "I'm not sure, Dad," she answered honestly. "I know my evidence is circumstantial. But I've got a terrible feeling that Bess is in danger from Richard Munro, and I can't ignore that. Please, would you call the police? Ask them to check at Bloom's and at Richard's home address and pick him up."

"On what grounds should they take him in?" her father asked. "For reading legal cases? That's hardly a criminal offense."

"Tell them he's our prime suspect," Nancy said. "That's enough to hold him for questioning. Just until we find out where Bess is and get her back safely. Please, Dad!"

Mr. Drew sighed. "All right, Nan," he said. "I'll ask the police to look for Richard Munro. But if we don't find some solid evidence of a crime, they won't be able to hold him for long."

Standing outside Bess's house, Nancy rang the doorbell for the third time. "I don't think anyone's home," she said to George, who stood beside her.

"The house is awfully quiet, and her parents' car isn't in the drive."

George fished out her key ring from her backpack. "Then let's go in," she said. "My aunt and uncle won't mind."

A few minutes later Nancy and George were sitting in front of the computer screen in Mr. Marvin's study. Nancy turned on the computer and waited impatiently while it booted up. She felt relieved as she saw that the Marvins used software that she was familiar with.

She started by searching a list of directories. One of them was titled BESS. "That must be her stuff," Nancy said, calling up the directory.

George glanced through the list of files. "Fall clothes that she wants to buy, makeup that she has to replace, restaurants she wants to go to . . ."

Nancy tried another file. "This file looks like recipes, all of them involving chocolate. And this one"—she displayed another file—"is more of those awful poems."

George winced. "I hate to say it, but we really should look at the poems," she said. "Maybe we'll find some sort of clue about Richard."

"You're right," Nancy agreed. "Here's one called 'My Dear Richard.' Let's see—his eyes are like emeralds, his lips like raspberry sherbet—"

"I'll never eat a raspberry again," George said with a moan.

"I know what you mean," Nancy agreed. She scrolled through the files more rapidly. "There isn't anything here about her date this morning."

George frowned. "This doesn't make sense," she said. "Bess was talking about their great literary correspondence, how she was saving all of Richard's letters for posterity. So how come we can't find any of their letters?"

"Why don't we try the e-mail directory?" Nancy said. She swiftly entered the program. She studied its setup for a minute, then said, "There's something called an Out Basket. Maybe that's where Bess puts the messages she sends out." Nancy opened the Out Basket, only to find it empty.

"Maybe Bess doesn't save the letters she sends to Richard," George mused. "Maybe she composes them on screen and sends them right out, without keeping a copy. She only saves *his* letters and expects him to save *hers*."

"That sounds very Bess," Nancy agreed. "Let's check the In Basket." She called up the files in the In Basket. "This may be it," she said excitedly. "The earliest one is dated Thursday—that's the day Cyril gave Bess Richard's e-mail address."

"Are all the messages from Richard?" George asked.

"All I can tell is that they're from the same computer address," Nancy said.

"This is strange, Nan," George said. "I feel like we're reading someone's mail."

"We are," Nancy assured her. She punched up one of the letters. "This one is signed THE BARD."

"She said that's how Richard signs his letters,"

George recalled, peering at the screen. "And look, he's telling Bess how exciting her poetry is. It's from Richard, all right."

Nancy scrolled farther down the letter. "Bess must have been sending him more than poetry," she noted. "He says something about hoping she'll enjoy seeing Sather's workshop."

George snapped her fingers. "That's how he knew where you were," George declared. "Bess was keeping him posted!"

Nancy realized with a sinking feeling that George had to be right. She quickly pulled up a second letter, then a third. All were from Richard Munro, and all mentioned somewhere Nancy had gone to investigate. The third letter ended, "Let me know what your plans are for tomorrow. Everything about you—even your friends—fascinates me. —THE BARD."

"This is getting really creepy," George said, wrapping her arms around herself. "He was spying on us through Bess."

"We still need to know where they went this morning," Nancy reminded George as she brought up the most recent letter on the screen.

The main part of the letter dealt with poetry. But in the last paragraph Nancy found what she was looking for.

"So we'll meet tomorrow morning at Bloom's," it said. "I'll open the store, and we'll have the coffee bar all to ourselves. Just you and me and the spirits of the great writers surrounding us."

George shuddered. "That sounds creepy—the

two of them and lots of dead writers. You know, I think this great romance has gone far enough."

Nancy nodded grimly. "Let's go to Bloom's," she said, punching keys to shut off the computer. "My father must have told the police what's happening by now. I want to be there when they arrive. Richard Munro has already tried to kill me. We have to get there before he tries to kill Bess, too!"

13

Who Is the Dark Lady?

Armed with the information from Bess's e-mail, Nancy and George hurried out of the Marvins' house and jumped into George's car. As George drove as fast as possible to Bloom's, Nancy hoped her dad had been able to convince the police to get to the store immediately. If Richard Munro was as dangerous as she suspected, she and George could very well need some backup.

"Nan," George said uneasily. "Do you think it's possible that Bess and Richard are just having a really good time on a date?"

"It's possible," Nancy admitted. "But not likely. I always thought it was weird that Richard never really acted interested in Bess in person. I don't trust him at all."

Nancy clung to the dashboard as George turned a sharp corner. Richard had arranged to meet Bess early at Bloom's, when it was still closed. By now the store would be open. Would Bess still be there? Or had Richard taken her somewhere else—somewhere deadly?

George turned onto Main Street. "Look, George!" Nancy said, pointing toward Bloom's. "There's a police cruiser parked in front. They *did* come."

"Thank goodness," George said. "Now, if we can just find a place to park this car . . ." But Bloom's parking lot was full, and by the time George and Nancy had parked down the street and jogged back to the store, the police cruiser was just pulling away.

"Wait!" Nancy cried, but the car didn't stop.

"Oh, no," George said. "It looks like we're on our own."

"And it looks like they didn't find Richard," Nancy said grimly. "He wasn't in that car."

Inside, the bookshop was crowded. Nancy searched through the crowd, but she didn't see Richard or Bess or Cyril. She went back to Cyril's office and knocked on the half-open door.

Cyril was sitting at his desk staring blankly at his computer, a worried frown on his face. He popped up brightly when he saw Nancy, a smile lighting his eyes. "Nancy! And George! What can I do for you two?"

"We're looking for Bess," Nancy said, trying to sound casual. "She was going to meet us here. Have you seen her? Or Richard?"

"Well, now," Cyril said, rubbing his chin, "I don't want to alarm you, but that's exactly what a police officer was in here asking a moment ago. All

I know is that Richard asked for the day off. There was talk of a picnic in the country, as I recall."

Nancy looked at George. There had been nothing in Richard's note about a picnic. Was that a cover story Richard had made up to tell Cyril? Or was it a surprise that Richard had in store for Bess?

"The police want to ask Richard some questions regarding the book thefts," Cyril went on in his friendly way. "If you do find those two lovebirds, would you please be so good as to tell them?"

"Of course," Nancy said. "Sorry to bother you."

"No bother," Cyril said warmly as the girls left.

"That's strange," George whispered as they started back toward the main part of the store. "Cyril didn't seem at all worried that the police are searching for Richard."

"No," Nancy agreed. "He seemed almost cheerful about it. I want to have a better look around Bloom's. Can you create a distraction?"

"No problem, Nan," George said, her gaze shifting across the room as she planned what to do next.

Suddenly George turned and crashed heavily into a table display about ten feet from Cyril's door. Stumbling to the ground, she cried out, "My ankle! Ouch!" The table went down, sending pyramids of books flying.

"Are you all right?" Cyril cried, running out of his office. In a moment's time several staff people had hurried to George's aid.

Nancy went into action, ducking behind the counter and then slipping toward the very back of the store. She slid through a door marked Employees Only and into a hallway. On one side was a stock room and a rest room. At the end of the hallway was another door.

Halfway down the hallway, Nancy saw something lying on the floor. She ran over to pick it up.

It was Bess's pink hair bow! That proved that Bess had been back this way. But when and why? Nancy felt her throat constrict with fear. Had Bess run back here to hide for some reason? Or had someone brought her here by force?

Nancy opened the door at the end of the hall and was faced with complete darkness. She took her flashlight out of her purse and aimed it into the dark, making out a flight of stairs. She closed the door carefully behind her so it wouldn't make a noise, then started down the stairway. The steps were solid marble, and she had to tiptoe so she wouldn't be heard. It was chilly in the lower reaches of the old bank building, and not a sound could be heard from the store up above.

In the basement dozens of rough bookshelves held cartons of books. Nancy moved her flashlight through the bookcase aisles, but there was no further sign that Richard or Bess had passed that way. Standing alone in the depths of the old bank, she wondered if she was on the right trail at all.

She turned her flashlight toward the boxes on the shelves. The upstairs stockroom had held new books, but a glance in several open boxes told her that old books were stored here. Were these Cyril's rare books? Nancy wondered.

Then she recalled hearing Risa Palmetto talking to Cyril that first day Nancy had visited Bloom's. "How could anyone get into that fancy vault of yours?" Risa had asked Cyril.

Where was that vault? Nancy wondered. Did Richard know about it? Was he stashing the stolen books there?

Nancy ran her flashlight over the basement's walls until a gleam of metal caught her eye. She stepped between two bookshelves to see what it was.

She reached out and touched a heavy bank vault door, set flush into a thick plaster wall. The metal was cold to touch, and Nancy pulled her hand away. The door looked old, as if made in the early years of the century, when the bank was first built. But someone had installed a new computerized keypad system on the lock.

Nancy tried the door. It was locked tight. She trained her flashlight on the computer keypad. Like the one at Rendell's, the keypad had letters. No doubt this one operated with a password, too.

Nancy sat back on her heels and thought. What kind of password would Cyril Bloom use? Maybe it was a simple one that the store employees also knew, something easy to remember so the staff could open the door, too. She tried punching in CYRIL and BLOOM. Neither one worked. Then she tried words like BANK, BOOK, and POETRY. Still no luck. Remembering how Richard had signed his letters to Bess, she tried BARD. No go.

Nancy sighed, frustrated. The code could be

anything at all—the name of Cyril's mother or even his third-grade teacher. It was a pretty long shot that she might actually figure it out.

Then Nancy thought of Bess. She couldn't give up, not if Bess needed her! I've got to use my imagination, Nancy told herself, just as Bess would. Now, how would Bess's mind work if she were in this situation?

"I've got it," Nancy whispered excitedly, remembering the book of Cyril's poems that Bess had told her about. With fresh resolve, Nancy eagerly punched in DARKLADY.

Nancy held her breath. To her amazement, the lock clicked open. A green light and a red light both lit beneath the keypad. Letting her breath out, Nancy gingerly pushed open the door, hoping that she hadn't set off some kind of silent alarm.

Leaving the door ajar, she stepped inside the vault. She swung her flashlight beam around. The vault room was larger than she'd expected. It even held bookcases and furniture: a table and some chairs and a long divan with something on top.

Nancy gasped as she pointed her flashlight at the divan. The something on top was Bess, gagged and bound!

"Bess!" Nancy cried.

"Mmflignphmp!" Bess mumbled through her gag.

"Just a minute," Nancy said. "I'm going to turn on the light, and then I'll untie you."

It took Nancy a good five minutes to untie her friend. Finally Bess was free. For a moment she just sat rubbing her wrists and ankles where the ropes had bit into her flesh. "It feels like pins and needles all over," she said in a shaky voice.

"That will go away when your circulation comes back," Nancy promised her. "Who did this to you?"

"Cyril!" Bess sputtered indignantly.

"Cyril?" Nancy echoed. "Why would Cyril tie you up and hide you down here?"

"I don't know," Bess said miserably. "He showed up this morning when I was waiting for Richard. He offered to let me into the store. Before I knew it, I was tied up down here—locked up with the Dark Lady!"

"What do you mean?" Nancy asked.

Bess pointed to a huge oil painting on the wall behind Nancy. "Remember the poetry Cyril wrote when he was young, all of it dedicated to a mysterious Dark Lady?" she said. "Well, there she is. Don't you recognize her?"

Nancy looked again at the portrait. It showed a young woman with long, dark windblown hair and suntanned skin. She was standing on a beach, wearing faded jeans and a white lace-trimmed Victorian blouse.

"Cyril has another picture of her, a photograph, on his desk," Bess said. She gave a rueful smile. "I noticed it when I was playing Love Detective. I did a little asking around, and late yesterday night I figured out who she was."

"Lily Truscott," Nancy said slowly. She recognized the woman as the same one she'd seen in the photograph Arianne had shown her.

Bess nodded. "I was going to call you and tell you, but first I sent Richard an e-mail message," she said. "I told him I'd figured out the Dark Lady was Lily, and he answered right away, very excited. That's when he made our date for breakfast, and I was so thrilled I completely forgot to tell you my news."

Nancy felt a chill go through her. "That's why Cyril tied you up down here," she said. "Richard must have told him that you figured out his connection to Lily."

Bess looked confused. "Why would Cyril care that I found out he once loved Lily Truscott?" she asked. "I'm sure he was devastated when she died, but that was so many years ago."

"Don't you see, Bess?" Nancy said. "This connects Cyril to the stolen books! We know that someone is trying to reassemble Lily Truscott's collection. Who would have more reason to do that than the man who loved her? Cyril is our book thief!"

Nancy turned and ran her finger along the cracked spine of a nearby book. "Here's that edition of *A Boy's King Arthur* that was stolen from Risa," she said. "And here's the *Alice in Wonderland* that disappeared from Rendell's. These have to be Lily's books. I'll bet that there's a pinhole on line four of page four of every one of them."

Bess's eyes shone. "We cracked the case!"

"But we haven't ended it yet," Nancy said in a worried tone. "We shouldn't be down here talking. We've got to get to the police and tell them about this. And first we have to find a way out of the store without Cyril seeing us before he comes back for you."

Suddenly, Bess looked over Nancy's shoulder, and her eyes widened with alarm. A feeling of dread shot through Nancy. She turned slowly.

Cyril Bloom was standing in the open doorway of the vault. He had one arm around George. His other hand held a knife pressed against her throat.

"I'm sorry, ladies," he said. "I believe it's much too late to escape me now."

14

Locked In!

Nancy stared at the knife gripped in Cyril's hand, only an inch away from George's throat. George looked as if she was taking it all relatively calmly, but Nancy knew that her friend rarely let her fear show. Cyril gave George a little nudge, and she stepped into the vault.

"Find anything interesting?" Cyril asked Nancy. "I must say, you *are* quite good at uncovering things, Miss Drew."

"You let George go!" Bess ordered. "Richard will be here any second with the police."

"What makes you so sure of that?" Cyril asked.

"Richard and I had a date this morning," Bess said. "I know he's searching all over town for me right now. He'll rescue us."

"A date? Don't be ridiculous," Cyril snapped.

"What do you mean?" Bess asked indignantly. "Richard and I write to each other four and five

129

times a day. By now he must know something's wrong."

Cyril gave Bess a look of withering contempt. "You little fool," he said. "I'm the one you've been corresponding with. I'm the one who's been reading your wretched poetry. That e-mail address I gave you was *mine*. Richard Munro's never read so much as one word you've written. He barely even knows you're alive."

Nancy watched as Bess's face went rigid with disbelief. Then she saw George swiftly drive her elbow backward into Cyril's stomach. "You disgusting slime!" George spat the words at Cyril.

Cyril doubled over with a gasp. George whirled, smashing an elbow into his shoulder so hard that he stumbled sideways.

"Let's get out of here," Nancy said, leaping for the open vault door.

But Bess seemed rooted in place. "Richard didn't care about me?" she said in an eerie, quiet tone. "He never read my poems? He never wrote to me at all?"

"Bess, we'll talk about this later," George shrieked from the vault doorway. "Let's go!"

But Bess was too stunned to move from her spot.

Nancy grabbed Bess's arm, but she wasn't fast enough. With a lightning movement, Cyril sprang up from the floor, still clutching the knife in his hand. This time it was Bess he grabbed.

Pressing the knife against Bess's throat, Cyril looked at Nancy and George. "I *will* cut her if either of you tries anything," he promised. "Unfortunately, your poetic friend here knows more than she should."

"You mean she figured out that Lily Truscott was the Dark Lady," Nancy said. "That's why you kidnapped her, isn't it? You didn't want anyone to know your secret, especially when you're so close to completing Lily's library."

"I loved Lily," Cyril said simply. "I was the only one who understood how much she loved those books. Next week is the twentieth anniversary of Lily's death. After she died, I vowed that I'd get all her beautiful books back together, even if it took me twenty years. The twenty years are nearly up." Cyril gripped the knife at Bess's throat so tightly that his knuckles turned white. "I must fulfill my vow in time!" he said in a ragged, desperate voice.

Nancy listened to Cyril with growing alarm. He was sick, she realized. He must have gone quietly crazy over the last twenty years. She knew she couldn't reason with a madman. Her only hope was to keep him talking until somehow she could get Bess free. "Why didn't you just buy back Lily's books?" Nancy asked Cyril as calmly as possible.

"I did buy many of them," Cyril replied. "But do you know how much the value of those books has risen over the past ten years? I already have two mortgages on my house to pay for all of this. Besides, some collectors refused to part with certain titles, and the same was doubly true of libraries. I didn't start out being a thief. If I could get a book honestly, I bought it."

"But if not, you stole it," George finished.

Cyril shrugged.

Bess suddenly spoke up as if she'd snapped out of a trance. "I still want to know about Richard," she said. "How much does he know about all of this?"

Cyril gave a low laugh. "Richard Munro doesn't want to know," he said. "Richard's a young, selfish man who wants only fame and money. He does odd jobs for me and doesn't ask questions."

"For example," Nancy said, "he researches ways to break security systems."

"He didn't read those books. He was just returning them to the library for me," Cyril said.

"So what are you going to do now?" George asked.

Cyril pressed the knife even more tightly against Bess's throat. "Well, that is a question," he admitted. "Fortunately, I have a nest egg." He reached behind Bess and removed a thick leather-bound volume from the shelf. "This book never belonged to Lily," he explained. "I, shall we say, *liberated* it from a private collector some years ago. Its sale will allow me to live very well for a while."

"What is that book?" George asked.

"It's an edition of Chaucer's *Canterbury Tales,* published by William Morris at the turn of the century," Cyril said. "In book circles it's known as a Kelmscott Chaucer. The illustrations are glorious woodcuts. It's a book collector's dream."

"You're going to sell it and go into hiding?" Nancy asked.

"For now," Cyril said, edging back toward the door with Bess still in his grasp, "all you need to know is that I'm going to leave you two here for a while."

George pulled a book from the shelf. "You trust us with your precious books?" she asked in an ominous tone. "What if we trash every book in this room?"

"If even one book is harmed, you'll never see your friend Bess again," Cyril promised.

George quickly put the book back on the shelf.

"We won't hurt the books," Nancy assured Cyril. "Just don't hurt Bess."

"I'm afraid that depends on how cooperative everyone else is," Cyril replied. He shoved Bess roughly through the open vault door. "If you get bored, girls, I suggest you read a book."

Then the vault door slammed shut.

Nancy ran to the door and pulled on the handle. It was locked and wouldn't budge.

"The store's full of people upstairs," George pointed out. "We could scream our heads off."

"It wouldn't do any good," Nancy said. "The vault walls are so thick, they'd never hear us." She looked around the windowless vault. Air vents led in, but they were no larger than Nancy's fist. As far as she could see, there was only one way out—through the locked door.

She turned her attention to the door. On the inside, the vault had another computer keypad lock mechanism. Nancy punched in DARKLADY.

Nothing happened. Obviously the inside password was different from the outside one.

"We have to figure out Cyril's password," Nancy told George. "The code on the outside of the vault was DARKLADY. But what other password could Cyril have programmed in here?"

George picked up one of Cyril Bloom's books of poetry, which had been lying on an end table. "Maybe we'll find something in here," she said. "There are four of his books here."

"You take two and I'll take two," Nancy suggested. "Look for anything that might be a password."

The girls spent two long, frustrating hours poring over Cyril's books and trying every word combination they could think of. The clock on the vault's wall clicked away. Nancy felt ill with worry whenever she stopped to wonder where Bess was.

Finally she threw down the book she was studying. "This is getting us nowhere," she declared.

George sank back on the divan, looking frightened. This worried Nancy more than anything. She'd almost never seen George look frightened.

"Don't worry," Nancy said, trying to keep her own tone calm. "The police will be looking for us. My dad knew we thought Bess was in danger, and he'll call them if we don't come home. And he's sure to tell them to check here at the bookstore."

"But what if Cyril comes back first?" George asked. "He's bound to come back. I'm sure he won't leave his precious library behind."

"No, he won't," Nancy had to admit. "My guess is that he'll get a truck and come back for his library after the store is closed, when no one's around."

"But what will he do with *us* then?" George asked in a small voice. "The guy's crazy, remember."

"We just have to hope that the police get here first," Nancy said firmly. "Or that we figure out that password."

Nancy turned her attention to the shelves. On one shelf were a row of hardbound diaries. Nancy picked one at random and opened it. It was written in Lily Truscott's old-fashioned script. "This writing is definitely Lily's," Nancy said. "But why was that threat written to me in the same writing?"

"Maybe Cyril's so obsessed with Lily, he learned to mimic her writing," George suggested.

"You're probably right," Nancy said. "These journals obviously mean a lot to Cyril. Maybe we can find a password in one of them."

Nancy pulled a couple of Lily's diaries off the shelf. As she did, she noticed a hollow space behind the bookshelf. She pushed aside more of the diaries. "George, I think I've found something!" she exclaimed.

George ran over as Nancy shone her flashlight on the hollow area. "There are hinges back here!" Nancy announced. "This shelf is designed to swing out—like a secret door."

135

The hinges were wedged between the wall and a fat book at the end of the top shelf. Nancy reached up for the book—and discovered it wasn't a book at all. It was a block of wood, painted to look like a copy of Shakespeare's tragedies. As she touched it, the false book tipped over on a spring, releasing a latch—and the whole bookshelf swung open!

Behind it she saw an old-fashioned wooden door, clearly part of the original old bank vault. Cyril must have built the hinged bookshelf to hide it. Heart racing, Nancy turned the knob and pushed.

Both girls held their breath as the door creaked open on rusty hinges. Behind it, Nancy could see a winding flight of metal stairs climbing upward.

"I don't believe it," George said.

"Neither do I, but let's go!" Nancy declared. She stopped only long enough to grab some evidence—the *Alice in Wonderland* that had been stolen from Rendell's. Then the girls quickly climbed the narrow spiral stairway.

At the top of the stairs was a door. Nancy pushed it open carefully. It led into Cyril Bloom's office, empty now and quiet. Nancy stepped into Cyril's office cautiously, with George following close behind.

"Something's wrong," Nancy whispered. "The store should be open at this hour, right? Why is it so quiet?"

George slipped over to peek out of the office door. "The lights are off, and there's no one there," she reported. "Cyril must have shut the store down."

"I don't like this," Nancy said. She moved quickly to Cyril's desk and picked up the phone. There was no dial tone. "The lines have been cut," she said. "Let's try the doors."

They ran through the deserted store to the front entrance. But the heavy doors were locked up tight with secure, modern deadbolt locks. A sign was taped to the front window: Closed early due to a gas leak. Our apologies—Cyril Bloom.

They checked a back door leading into the alley. It was locked, too. Even the windows were locked and required a key to be opened.

"We can stand in the front window," George suggested. "Maybe we could catch the attention of someone walking down the street."

"I have a more direct solution," Nancy told her. She picked up a small antique table, strode over to the nearest window, and hurled the table with all her strength. The plate glass cracked, though it didn't break. The store's alarm began to shriek.

"Hit it again!" George shouted above the piercing sound. "Break it open and I'll climb through."

Nancy shook her head and smiled at her friend. "All I wanted was to call the police," she said. "This ought to bring them here, don't you think?"

The police quickly showed up to check out the alarm. Nancy didn't know either of the cops who first arrived, but she asked them to call Officer

Nomura, who soon arrived and confirmed that Nancy and George were not thieves. A locksmith was brought to open the deadbolt locks. By the time the doors were opened, Lieutenant Walker had joined them as well.

While the other officers investigated the cache of stolen books in the vault below, Nancy filled Nomura and Walker in on what had happened.

"We'll have to proceed carefully," Lieutenant Walker said when she had finished. "Bloom is armed, and he has a hostage. If we make a wrong move, Bess could be in serious trouble. Do you have any idea where he might go?"

"In fact, I do," said Nancy. "He took a valuable book with him, something called a Kelmscott Chaucer. He was bragging that he could get a lot of money for it. I think he's trying to sell it quick."

Officer Nomura asked, "Where would he go to sell such an expensive book?"

"He needs cash," Lieutenant Walker pointed out. "I bet he'd sell it to someone who could come up with cash immediately and not ask too many questions."

Nancy snapped her fingers. "I know someone who might be able to help us—a book dealer I met, William Laws. I have his card in my purse." Nancy took out her wallet and handed Laws's card to Walker.

"Why don't you call him, he knows you," the lieutenant said. He handed Nancy a portable phone, and she punched in Laws's number.

"Of course I'll help," William Laws said when Nancy had explained the situation. "I know a few places where Cyril might sell that book. Let me make some calls and find out if Cyril has contacted anyone. These people are more likely to talk to me than to you or the police."

Nancy, George, and the police detectives waited an anxious half hour. Finally, the lieutenant's portable phone rang.

"I've found your man," William Laws told Nancy. "I phoned a collector named Everett Gould, and ten minutes after I called him, Cyril phoned him up, offering him a Kelmscott Chaucer for sale. Gould told Cyril he was interested and then immediately called me back. He's willing to cooperate with the police. He understands that Cyril is dangerous."

"That's terrific," Nancy said. "Give me his number, and I'll have the police call him right now."

"There's just one thing, Nancy," Mr. Laws said. "When Cyril called Gould, he said, 'My wife and I will bring the Chaucer to you.' I know Cyril never married. Could he be talking about your friend Bess?"

Nancy felt her mouth go dry. "I'm afraid so," she said. "We'll have to figure out how to approach Cyril without scaring him off or giving him any reason to hurt Bess."

"He sounds like a desperate man," Laws said.

Nancy agreed. "There must be a way to get Bess

out of harm," she said, shutting her eyes tight as she frantically searched her mind for an idea. A vision of the knife at Bess's throat came to Nancy, and she shuddered.

Suddenly she opened her eyes and said, "I've got it! I think what we need here is a sting."

15

The Sting

"A sting?" Mr. Laws asked. George and the police detectives looked at her curiously.

"Right, a hoax," Nancy explained to Mr. Laws as well as the others. "Suppose Everett Gould tells Cyril he does want to buy that Chaucer book. Cyril and Bess will show up at Gould's to make the sale. Cyril will be pretending Bess is his wife."

George nodded, and the police and Law listened as Nancy continued.

"He can't exactly hold a gun to her head in front of Gould," she said. The police caught on to Nancy's idea, and soon they had worked out all the details.

"It'll be tough to pull it off," Nancy said. "But you know, it just might work."

Early that evening Nancy sat in Everett Gould's spare bedroom, her hands clenched tight with tension. Across the room sat Lieutenant Walker and Officer Nomura, both equally tense. Cyril Bloom was due to arrive any minute. They hoped Bess would be with him.

The bedroom door had been propped open a crack so that they could watch what was going on in Mr. Gould's library. Two other cops were hidden in the kitchen, and officers in unmarked cars were parked outside.

Mentally, Nancy rehearsed the plan. If Bess arrived with Cyril, Gould would do his best to distract Cyril, while Nancy tried to get Bess's attention and make her run for safety. Then the police could apprehend Cyril without endangering Bess.

If Bess wasn't with Cyril, the police would let him complete the sale and then follow him, hoping that he'd lead them to Bess.

Lieutenant Walker had given Gould an envelope of marked bills. Gould seemed nervous but determined to play his part well. Everything was ready.

Nancy looked down at her clenched fingers, released them, and took a deep, steadying breath. She knew she needed to keep a clear head now. But how could she help but worry while her friend was in Cyril Bloom's hands?

Officer Nomura's pocket radio squawked. She spoke into it, then said, "Bloom's car has been spotted. He has Bess Marvin with him."

Nancy felt her heart pound faster with anxiety.

After what seemed like an endless wait, she heard the doorbell ring and Gould go to answer it.

A few seconds later, she could see Gould leading his visitors into the library.

Bess was there!

Cyril had his hand on her arm. It looked companionable, but Nancy noticed the way his fingers gripped her flesh. Bess looked pale and frightened. Even Mr. Gould appeared anxious now. His large afghan hound, who had trailed them into the library, seemed uneasy, too. Oh, please don't let them blow it, Nancy wished silently.

"My wife isn't feeling well," she heard Cyril explain to Gould.

"Why don't you have a seat?" Gould said to Bess.

"She feels better standing, don't you, Sally?" Cyril answered for Bess, his handsome face full of concern. Nancy noted what a smooth actor Cyril was. He certainly had fooled her for a long time.

"I really must get my wife home," Cyril said. "I hope you'll understand that I need to make this transaction quickly."

"Of course," Gould said. His eyes darted sideways toward the spare bedroom door. Then he reached for the package Cyril was offering him.

Cyril held on to the package. "You do understand the terms of this transaction?" he said. "Cash and no questions asked."

"I do," Gould assured him. "I have the money right here in my desk. But I can't turn over such a large amount until I've inspected the volume."

A flash of impatience crossed Cyril's face, and

then it was gone. "Of course," he said mildly. But Nancy could see his grip tighten on Bess's arm, and Bess seemed to be gritting her teeth. Nancy felt for her friend.

Gould made a big production of carefully opening the book's brown paper wrapping. He was stalling for time. There was nothing they could do as long as Cyril held Bess so close.

Drop the book, Mr. Gould, Nancy urged him silently. Just follow the plan and drop the book.

As though he had heard her, Gould suddenly dropped the precious volume he had just unwrapped.

Cyril lunged for it, shouting, "What's the matter with you? That's a twenty-five-thousand-dollar book!"

Gould kicked at Cyril's hand. The dog, following his master's lead, snarled and pounced at Cyril. As Cyril dropped Bess's arm and tumbled to the ground, Nancy screamed, "Bess, it's Nancy! Run this way!"

Reacting swiftly, Bess raced into the spare bedroom. She hugged Nancy tightly as the police officers stepped out into the library.

In a few more minutes it was all over. Cyril was led to a waiting police car. Still shaken and pale, Bess sat down while a police officer brought her a glass of water.

Everett Gould stood alone at his desk, his dog curled protectively at his feet. Gould stared numbly down at the stolen Chaucer. Nancy crossed the room to speak to him. "We're so grateful for your

144

help, Mr. Gould," she said sympathetically. "It must have been unnerving to have police in your bedroom, a man with a hostage in your living room—"

"It wasn't that," Gould said, shaking his head. "It wasn't that at all. For the first time in my life I was actually holding a Kelmscott Chaucer, and I dropped it. I deliberately dropped it." He shook his head in disbelief.

The next afternoon Nancy, George, and Bess arrived at Leonard Sather's workshop. Nancy had spent the morning at the police station, answering questions and getting some answers of her own. Now it was her turn to share that information with the friends who'd helped her solve the case.

"We'll have tea and pastries upstairs in my place," Lori said as she greeted them at the door. "Leonard's got a rule about no food in the workshop."

Upstairs Nancy found Arianne Stone sitting crosslegged on the braided rug in Lori's apartment. Leonard Sather was sitting across from her in an armchair.

"I can't believe Cyril Bloom had a Kelmscott Chaucer for years and never let me see it," Leonard was saying. "He knew I'd give my eyeteeth to hold a book like that."

"I wish I'd had a chance to ask him about my aunt Lily," Arianne said. "There's so much I'd still like to know about her."

"Cyril might not be a very reliable source,"

Nancy warned. "He became totally fixated on Lily after she died. What he remembers might be more his imagination than the person who really existed."

Bess perched on the arm of Lori's chair. "What I still don't understand is that threatening note in Richard's poetry book," she said. "Wasn't that Lily's handwriting?"

"Cyril apparently even taught himself to duplicate Lily's handwriting," Nancy said. "He copied it from her old journals. When he wrote that message in my book that night, he used her handwriting."

"My aunt loved the nineteenth century so much, she taught herself to write in the style of the 1890s," Arianne added.

"She was so unusual," Bess said wistfully. "No wonder Cyril loved her so much."

"That wasn't love, it was obsession," George said. "Which explains why he was so determined to stop Nancy's investigation."

Nancy nodded. "Remember when you told him I was a detective, Bess?" she said. "He must have decided at once to scare me off the case. That's why he said he was giving you Richard's computer address—so he could keep track of what I was finding out."

"So he's the one who followed you here and punctured your exhaust pipe?" Leonard asked.

"That day I called home on my way here and told Hannah to tell Bess where I was going," Nancy said. "And Bess unwittingly told Cyril on e-mail. He'd already slashed my tire at the auction. He came out here to try a different way to throw me off his trail."

Leonard Sather poured himself a second mug of tea. "What I want to know," he said, "is how Cyril stole that book from Rendell's. They have quite a security system."

"I asked the police about that," Nancy said. "He used one of the techniques I read about in those law books. It's what they call a Trojan horse. When you set up a computer program, you can put in a 'failsafe'—a password that overrides everything else in the program.

"Mr. Rendell asked Cyril to help him enter the password that controlled the alarm system for the preview room," she went on. "Cyril entered one of their passwords and showed them how to change it. But first he secretly entered his own password, which would override anything they put in."

"So at the auction Cyril just tapped in his own password and walked right into the locked room?" George asked.

"Exactly," Nancy said. "The system was just waiting for him to break it. He stole the book during the auction when all the guards were watching over that manuscript that sold for thirteen thousand dollars. It only took him a minute to get in and out of that room."

"He sure was devious," George said with reluctant admiration. "He even had a secret stairway leading from his office to the vault."

"Lieutenant Walker says that stairway was always there," Nancy corrected her. "It was a common feature in banks of that time—a personal vault entrance for the bank owner, so he could check what was inside the vault. Cyril's office used to be the bank manager's."

"But back up a bit. How did Cyril steal all those other books?" Lori asked.

"He'd make friends with private collectors, take a look at their systems, then come back once he'd learned how to foil the system," Nancy said. "And when the police searched his house last night, they found all sorts of wax molds. He used to steal keys from library offices and counters, press them against the wax, replace the key before anyone noticed, and then have the keys made. They also found a half-dozen false and stolen faculty IDs for university libraries."

"So that's how he got into Emerson's rare book room," Arianne said softly.

Nancy nodded. "At a place like Emerson, he'd use an ID from another university, claiming he was a visiting professor," she explained. "That way no one at Emerson would realize his ID was false. He'd also wear disguises so he could go back to the same place more than once."

Lori gave Arianne a curious look. "So is everything okay with you at Emerson?" she asked.

"Yes, thanks to all of you," Arianne said. "The River Heights police called the library and told them about Cyril. Now I'm completely cleared, and I've got my library job back. In fact," she said, standing up, "I have to get back to campus. My shift starts in a couple of hours."

Arianne started for the door that led downstairs, then turned back. "I do have one more question, Nancy," she said. "What happens to Aunt Lily's books?"

"The stolen books will stay in police custody until Cyril's trial is over," Nancy said. "After that, they'll be returned to their owners. But Cyril legitimately owned most of Lily's library—he actually bought more books than he stole. I guess he'll store them somewhere until he's out of prison."

Arianne gave Nancy a wry smile. "Well, maybe one day I'll be in a position to get some of Aunt Lily's books back—legally!" With a wave, she skipped down the stairs. A minute later they all heard the rumble of her motorcycle starting up outside.

"So all the stolen books were recovered?" Leonard Sather asked.

"All but two," Nancy said. "But Cyril's *Peter Pan* book wasn't really stolen. That was just another one of his lies. He said it was stolen so that no one would suspect him of being the thief. The truth was, it was one of Lily's books he had bought. He never intended to sell it—to Risa or anyone else."

"And your *Hound of the Baskervilles?*" George asked.

Nancy blushed. "Actually, that's the one missing book that Cyril didn't steal," she admitted.

"No one stole it. Hannah found it behind some other books on the top shelf of the hall bookcase. It was safe at home all along."

Lori, George, and Mr. Sather chuckled with Nancy. But looking over at Bess, Nancy noticed that she wasn't joining in. "What is it, Bess?" she asked.

"I can't help it," Bess said. "I'm wondering what will happen to Richard now."

"The police picked him up last night," Nancy said. "He'll be charged with being an accomplice. But from what they can tell, he knew so little about what Cyril was doing, he'll probably get off."

Bess sat back, looking relieved.

"Bess, I really should thank you," Nancy said.

"Me? For what?"

"For solving some very tough puzzles in this case," Nancy said. "Without you and your imagination, I don't know if we would ever have found out who our book burglar was. You found the pinhole that none of us noticed. You were the one who figured out who the Dark Lady was. And if you hadn't been talking about the Dark Lady so often, I never would have thought of using her name to open the vault."

"And you guys are always telling me I have an overactive imagination," Bess teased.

"This is one time it came in handy," George admitted.

"I wonder what will happen to the store," Bess said wistfully. "I'm going to miss Bloom's. Maybe I should run a coffeehouse-bookstore. I could serve my double-chocolate devil's food cake. And I could stock the store with lots of romances. Cyril didn't have a very good romance section. And I could run poetry readings—"

Nancy and George's eyes met. They both said, *"No more poetry! Ever!"*

Bess looked hurt for a second, then laughed good-naturedly. "Never mind," she said. "It was just an idea."

Nancy Drew®

www.NancyDrew.com

Online Mysteries and Official Nancy Drew Website

- Help Nancy solve original interactive online mysteries

- Online club and weekly email newsletter

**Do your younger brothers and sisters
want to read books like yours?**

**Let them know there
are books just for *them!***

They can join Nancy Drew and her best
friends as they collect clues and solve
mysteries in

THE

NANCY DREW

NOTEBOOKS®

Starting with

#1 The Slumber Party Secret
#2 The Lost Locket
#3 The Secret Santa
#4 Bad Day for Ballet

AND

**Meet up with suspense and mystery
in The Hardy Boys® are: The Clues Brothers™**

Starting with

#1 The Gross Ghost Mystery
#2 The Karate Clue
#3 First Day, Worst Day
#4 Jump Shot Detectives

A MINSTREL® BOOK

Published by Pocket Books

2324